CHEERLEADERS®

#18

LOOKING GOOD

CAROL ELLIS

D1487934

SCHOLASTIC INC.
New York Toronto London Auckland Sydney

ISBN 0-590-40188-2

12 11 10 9 8 7 6 5 4 3 2 1   6   6 7 8 9/8 0 1/9

CHEERLEADERS®

LOOKING GOOD

CHEERLEADERS

CHAPTER

Olivia Evans stepped into a pair of soft corduroy pants, pulled a warm rust-colored turtleneck over her head, and walked up to the mirror of the Tarenton High girls' locker room. As she ran a brush through her reddish-brown hair, she glanced over at Nancy Goldstein, who was sharing the mirror space. Nancy was brushing her hair, too, which was a big waste of energy as far as Olivia was concerned. She could count on the fingers of one hand the number of times she'd seen Nancy's thick, dark hair in any condition less then perfect.

For a moment, the only sound was the crackle of winter-dry hair being coaxed into place. Olivia finally broke the silence. "You won't believe this, but I think I'd rather face my mother right now than go back in that gym and face Ardith."

Nancy's dark eyes flickered with amusement.

1

Even though Olivia had recovered fully — if her athletic ability was any indication — from a serious childhood heart ailment, she still had to battle an overprotective mother who dogged her every step with a handful of tissues and a mouthful of warnings about overexertion, bad weather, and germs.

"You're right," Nancy said. "I don't believe you. But I know what you mean." She flicked a piece of lint from the shoulder of her cable-knit sweater. "Ardith's really going to let us have it."

Olivia and Nancy were members of Tarenton High's Varsity Cheerleading Squad, and Ardith Engborg was their coach. A dynamic, demanding, exacting leader, Ardith didn't expect perfection from her squad — she simply expected the cheerleaders to aim for it. If they tried and failed, she'd be fair; if they didn't try, she'd be furious. Lately, they hadn't been trying.

"What's wrong with us, anyway?" Olivia asked Nancy's reflection. "I mean, nobody fell on their face tonight, nobody really goofed up, but it felt like we were — "

"Like we were sleepwalkers," Nancy finished. "Or robots. Just going through the motions."

"I can think of a few motions I'd like to go through right now." Angie Poletti's smiling face joined the two grim ones in the mirror. "And they aren't cartwheels or back flips, either."

Olivia grinned. "Let me guess. Are they solo moves?"

"Definitely not," Angie said. "They have to be performed with a partner."

2

"A partner of the opposite sex?" Nancy said. "By the name of Christopher Page?"

Angie's smile widened. "Chris Page, Chris Page," she said. "Tall, blond, gorgeous? Is that who you mean?"

"Is there another one?" Nancy said dryly.

"And the moves you're talking about are tight ones, aren't they?" Olivia teased. "Lots of body contact, right?"

"Right!" Angie's glow deepened to a blush as she thought of Chris. She still couldn't believe that the most beautiful boy anyone had ever seen had actually singled her out for his attention. But he had, and the best part was that Christopher Page was more than gorgeous. He was sensitive, and loyal, and caring — qualities Angie loved even more than his great looks. Which was why, he'd told her, she was the girl for him.

Angie laughed again, bent forward from the waist, and vigorously applied a brush to the back of her head. "I think it's the weather," she said.

"You think what's the weather?"

"Why we've been so rotten lately." Angie straightened, peering through a curtain of blonde hair. Love might be blind, but she wasn't. She loved being a cheerleader, and was the squad's best all-around athlete and most loyal member. But she'd known for weeks that the cheerleaders were just "going through the motions," as Nancy put it, and it bothered her. "It has to be the weather," she went on. "I mean, it feels like

3

we've been slogging through slush and snow forever. And I haven't heard the weatherman talking about an early spring."

"Maybe you're right, Angie," Nancy said. "Maybe it is just a bad case of the winter blahs."

"Is there a cure?" Olivia asked.

"Yep." Angie grinned. "Boys."

"We've got that," Nancy pointed out, and for a moment the three girls laughed and forgot about the squad's problem. They were all very different in personality and appearance: Nancy was cool and stunningly pretty; Olivia, small, wiry, and very much her own person; Angie, wholesome, radiant, and genuinely friendly. For a moment, they shared more than the bond of being on the Varsity Squad; they shared the warm but sometimes unsettling feelings that came with loving a boy, and having that love returned.

Then Olivia brought them back to reality. "Somehow, I just don't think Ardith's going to buy the 'winter blahs' excuse."

"Buy it?" Nancy said. "She won't even listen to the sales pitch."

"You're right." Angie stuffed her brush into a canvas bag. "Well, maybe some time off is exactly what we need."

"Time off? Time off?" Olivia managed a good imitation of Ardith Engborg's voice. "What have you done to deserve time off, Angie Poletti? What have any of you done? You're as stale as week-old bread and just about as exciting. If you were Tarenton's basketball team instead of its cheerleading squad, you'd have lost that game tonight."

4

Olivia dropped the voice and sighed. "We might not have classes for a week, but you can bet we'll still be coming here — for practice."

"Livvie's right," Nancy agreed, and sighed, too. "We might as well go into the gym and get the lecture over with."

Angie nodded — it wasn't in her nature to sigh — and called out, "Mary Ellen? We're going to face the music now. Are you just about finished in there?"

The hiss of a shower stopped abruptly, and Mary Ellen Kirkwood's voice answered, "I'll be out in a couple of minutes."

Mary Ellen waited until she heard the door swish closed. Then she stepped out of the steamy shower stall, wrapped a well-worn towel around herself, and walked up to the mirror. Her vivid blue eyes, troubled and anxious, stared back. But the trouble wasn't a pimple on her flawless complexion, and the anxiety wasn't caused by the squad's distinct lack of zip.

Mary Ellen Kirkwood, the squad's captain, was as aware of the squad's problem as anyone. But she had something else on her mind at the moment. Her career, to be exact. More than anything, she wanted to be a fashion model, and if her reflection meant anything, she had what it would take. Her golden blonde hair fell in soft, silky waves around the beautifully chiseled bones of her face, and her figure, though partially obscured at the moment, was perfect.

What's more, Mary Ellen had determination. She'd wanted to make the Varsity Squad, and she had. She'd wanted to be on the honor roll every year, and she was. She wanted to model, and she was actually doing it, even though it was just a small job at the mall, standing on a platform outside a boutique. She did all those things, and she was equally determined to do more. She meant to break into the world of high-fashion modeling and make a name for herself in New York City, not in Tarenton. She meant to live in a spectacular high-rise apartment, not in a small, tacky, turquoise house. And she meant to earn enough money so her father wouldn't have to drive a bus and her mother wouldn't have to be a clerk.

She wanted to make it so big, Mary Ellen thought as she dried herself, that the only towel she'd ever use would be as thick as velvet, not a threadbare terrycloth thing she'd had for years.

Mary Ellen's goals were never farther away than the back of her mind. But what had brought them right up to the front again, what had put that anxious, troubled look in her eyes, was a letter that had arrived the day before, a letter she now pulled out of her duffle bag and read for perhaps the hundredth time:

Dear Miss Kirkwood,

As you can see from the letterhead, I am the director of the Futura Modeling Agency in Chicago.

Futura is always on the lookout for fresh young faces, and one of my assistants, having viewed the commercial your cheerleading

squad made for Clean Soap, brought yours
to my attention.

I contacted Harris Scheckner, the
commercial's producer, got your name from
him, and am writing to inquire whether you
would be available for an interview, in
our offices, at your earliest convenience.

Please understand that this would be an
exploratory interview; neither of us would be
bound to enter into any agreement, but we
do feel a meeting would be worth your while.

If you are interested, please let us know.
We look forward to hearing from you.

Best regards,
Martin Seltzman

Mary Ellen didn't really need to read the
letter again. She had it memorized. "If you are
interested." *If?* It was only what she'd been waiting for, working for, dreaming of, almost all her
life. Interested didn't begin to describe what she
was. Ecstatic was more like it.

But Mary Ellen was also practical. Maybe not
as practical as Nancy Goldstein, but practical
enough to know that the $175 she'd saved from
her job was ten dollars short of the roundtrip air-
fare. Her parents had absolutely no money to
spare. If she raided her little sister's piggy bank,
she could fly to Chicago and fly home, but how
would she eat? Okay, so she was willing to starve
for two days, but she refused to sleep on a park
bench. Besides, how would she even get to that
park bench from the airport?

She did have a little money a great-aunt had

left her, but Mary Ellen's mother insisted that money be left intact for dire emergencies.

Why did everything always come down to money? Why weren't looks and brains and ambition ever enough? If Mary Ellen had to turn down that interview, she knew she'd never get over the disappointment of having missed a big chance.

Well, she just wouldn't turn it down, that was all. Somehow, some way, she was going to Chicago. But first, she had to get chewed out by Ardith Engborg. She dressed, combed her hair, and went into the gym, wishing, as she did more often than she liked to admit, that she was the female counterpart to Preston Tilford III. He was good-looking and smart, like she was. There was one difference: Pres Tilford was rich.

The object of Mary Ellen's envy was, at that moment, feeling as dissatisfied as Mary Ellen, but for a different reason. Pres tried to look interested as Walt Manners, fresh from a shower in the boys' locker room, dug into his canvas carryall and pulled out, yard by yard, a green-and-orange-striped muffler.

"Think it'll make her laugh?" Walt asked.

"Make who laugh?"

"Olivia, who do you think?"

Pres stared at the muffler. It had to be at least six feet long, and the thought of it wrapped around Olivia Evans' slender neck made *him* laugh, at least. But it was hard to predict what Olivia's reaction to anything would be. "I don't know," he said finally. "Is that what you want to do? Make her laugh?"

"Sure." Walt's friendly, open face broke into a smile. "Not that she's down or anything. But I like to surprise her, see if I can get a grin out of her, you know?"

Pres nodded. "Where'd you get that thing, anyway?"

"My parents' show." Walt's mother and father hosted a morning television talk show from their home in the woods. They interviewed housewives and Senators, giants of industry and people on welfare. The Mannerses were liked and respected by their peers, but their son, Walt, though equally liked, remained untouched by the glamorous world of communications. He was stocky, as friendly as a puppy, and until he and Olivia had found each other, the kind of boy girls confided in about their problems with *other* boys. "Mom was interviewing this woman who runs some kind of home knitting business, and the lady left the scarf behind as a sample. When I saw it, I grabbed it. It's perfect for Olivia," he laughed. "She can fling it at her mother whenever Mrs. Evans starts freaking about the weather."

Pres laughed along, but his heart wasn't in it. He never thought he'd ever envy a guy like Walt Manners. Although, as he was the first to admit, Walt's clumsiness disappeared the minute he donned his cheerleading uniform. Then Walt displayed a graceful, effortless strength that always amazed Pres.

No, Pres envied Walt for having Olivia. Not

that Pres wanted Olivia. He liked her. He thought she was an incredibly gifted athlete and a pretty girl, but he didn't want her.

Preston Tilford III knew he could get just about any girl he wanted. All he had to do was rev the powerful engine of his red Porsche and flash his famous smile. Few girls — if any — would turn their backs on him.

But there weren't many girls he wanted to rev his engine for. At the moment, in fact, there weren't any. For a while, there had been Claudia. But she'd been too eager for him to follow in his father's footsteps and become, some fateful day, president of Tarenton Fabricators.

Pres didn't deny that he enjoyed money and everything it could buy, including his beloved Porsche. But he was determined not to spend his life behind a desk making that money, wearing a three-piece suit to the office on weekdays, and a preppy alligator shirt to the club on weekends.

Pres had different ideas about what business was all about. He had recently entered into an arrangement with Patrick Henley, Mary Ellen Kirkwood's sometime boyfriend. Pres and Patrick moved people, or, rather, they moved people's belongings, from house to house, office to office, apartment to apartment. The business was flourishing, and that made Pres happy.

What would have made him happier, though, was having a girl in his arms.

"Hey." Walt broke into Pres's thoughts. "You're not planning to hide in here, are you? Not that I blame you, but you know Ardith," he joked. "She'll track you down no matter where you are."

Pres pushed himself away from the bank of lockers. "You think she's mad at me, huh?"

"I think she's mad at all of us," Walt said. "There was definitely fire in the lady's eyes when she called a meeting after the game. Come on, let's go and get it over with."

As Pres followed Walt out of the locker room, he thought how much easier it would be to face Mrs. Engborg's fire if only he had a little fire of his own going.

Ardith Engborg sat on a bottom bleacher and watched her squad straggle into the gym. She was sure they expected a grand gripe session, on her part, and she was half inclined to give it to them. Technically, the squad hadn't been so bad lately, but they had absolutely no spirit, no fire, no oomph!

She couldn't pinpoint the problem. Nobody was going through a personal crisis that she knew of. But looking at the frown on Mary Ellen's face, Ardith thought she could detect one brewing. And there was Pres Tilford, pacing like a caged panther. The boy didn't need exercise, that much she knew. But she didn't know what he *did* need, except maybe a cold shower.

Well, Ardith thought, maybe that's the solution. It's been a long season and everybody, including me, is tired of the same old routine. Maybe a dash of ice-cold water in the face is exactly what we all need.

11

She smiled inwardly at what she was about to do, both for herself and for her squad. Then she clapped her hands once to get the group's attention.

"I'm sure I don't have to tell you that you've been performing like automatons lately." She watched the cheerleaders cringe, waiting for the usual groans and an onslaught of criticism. Then she went on quietly. "Anybody have any ideas as to the reason?"

Mary Ellen stared at her hands; Pres kept his eyes on some remote spot above Ardith's head; Angie giggled as Nancy nudged her in the arm.

"Go ahead," Nancy whispered. "Tell her your theory about the weather."

"You want to see her bite my head off?" Angie giggled again, but then stopped in surprise as Ardith said, "Well, if there's no specific reason, maybe it's just the winter blahs. I know I have them."

That got everybody's attention. No one could remember ever hearing Ardith Engborg admitting to a weakness, even a small one like the winter blahs.

"So here's my solution," Ardith went on. "We'll have a workout tomorrow as usual. Saturday's the game with Hillsborough, and Monday is the beginning of midyear recess." She paused and looked them over. "The following Monday is the game with Deep River, so we'll work out next Saturday. Enjoy the break."

The squad sat in surprised silence, until Ardith finally broke the quiet with a second clap of her hands. "That's it. See you tomorrow," she said, and watched as the six cheerleaders filed out of the gym like sleepwalkers, stunned by the news that their hard-driving coach was actually giving them a vacation.

CHAPTER

Mary Ellen trudged her way through the Tarenton High parking lot, ignoring the biting wind that tore at her hair. So what if her hair got tied in a thousand knots? If she couldn't get to Chicago, she didn't care what she looked like. Liar, she told herself. You always care what you look like. If you didn't, Mr. Seltzman from the Futura Modeling Agency would never have written that letter.

But right at that moment, she didn't care as much as she usually did. She wanted to go to Chicago so badly she could feel it, literally, right in the pit of her stomach. It wasn't a pleasant feeling; it hurt, and it pushed everything, including thoughts about her appearance, to the back of her mind.

Speaking of minds, Mary Ellen wondered briefly what was on Ardith's. Time off? She could hardly believe it, but she certainly wasn't going to turn down that precious gift. Now she had both the invitation to Chicago and the time to go; she hadn't even considered the time factor before. All she needed now, as usual, was the money.

The parking lot was almost empty, and normally that would have been just fine with Mary Ellen. She didn't like advertising the fact that she had no car, no way to get home except by bus. Today, though, with the bitter wind that tore the tears from her eyes and was probably putting a permanent chap on her cheeks, she would have swallowed her pride and begged a ride from almost anyone, just so she wouldn't have to stand around waiting for a poky, overheated bus filled with sweaty bodies.

She was thinking of Pres again, cruising along in his Porsche, no doubt, on the way to his fabulous lakefront house, when she saw the Chevy van with Patrick Henley behind the wheel. A moving van wasn't exactly her idea of a chariot, but it was a lot better than a garbage truck (Patrick's other means of transportation and income), and it beat riding the bus. She had to admit, too, that Patrick Henley, in spite of his annoying fondness for manual labor, was the most exciting boy she'd ever met.

Even bundled up and windblown, Mary Ellen Kirkwood was a beauty, and Patrick's eyes lit up when he saw her. Deftly maneuvering the van to the curb, he pushed open the passenger door and smiled at the only girl he'd ever wanted. "Need a lift, lady?"

"In more ways than one," Mary Ellen said.

She climbed gracefully into the van beside him, pulled the door closed, turned, and met Patrick's lips.

She hadn't been expecting the kiss, but that didn't matter. Dark-haired, dark-eyed Patrick was the only boy whose kisses could light a fire inside Mary Ellen, a fire that would never go out completely. She'd kissed other boys and enjoyed it, but the enjoyment never lasted much longer than the kiss itself. With Patrick, it was different. In fact, Patrick was different. Easily one of the best-looking boys at Tarenton High, he was bright, charming, funny, and sweet. He was the boy Mary Ellen could see herself spending the rest of her life with, except for one problem: Patrick owned a garbage truck and was proud of it.

A horn blared behind them, and Mary Ellen used it as an excuse to gently pull herself out of Patrick's arms. If only those arms didn't heave twenty-pound bags of trash into the back of a smelly truck, she would have gladly stayed in them and in Tarenton, maybe forever.

Patrick noticed the faint frown on Mary Ellen's forehead, and wondered, as he always did, why she refused to see how perfect they were for each other. Easing the van back onto the road, he said, "Don't tell me. That wasn't the kind of lift you had in mind, right?"

"It was perfect. And so's this," Mary Ellen said, indicating the van. "Thanks for giving me a ride. My toes were starting to get numb." She spoke quickly, not wanting to get into an argument. Her feelings were too confusing to analyze,

16

let alone defend. "Hey, guess what? Ardith's giving us almost the entire midyear recess off."

"No kidding? She sick or something?"

"I don't think so. Not unless she's sick of the squad, which she probably is." Mary Ellen eyed the beautiful homes across the lake, then watched as they drove past the neighborhood where Nancy Goldstein lived — not as exclusive as the lakefront property, but elegant just the same.

The closer they got to the Kirkwood home, the less Mary Ellen wanted to see. Shutting her eyes against the rows of small, drab houses, she leaned her head back as if she were tired. But her feet were tapping and her hands were clenched, and Patrick noticed her agitation.

"What is it, Mary Ellen?" he asked softly. "Is something wrong?"

Mary Ellen's stomach did a little flip at the sound of his voice, so full of concern for her. In the same instant, she had an idea. Maybe Patrick would loan her some money. You know he's saving every cent he has to buy a fleet of garbage trucks, one of her voices told her. So what? another voice said. It's only a loan. You'd pay him back.

Mary Ellen decided to go along with the second voice and see what happened. "It's this," she said. Mary Ellen pulled out Martin Seltzman's letter and read it aloud as Patrick drove her the rest of the way home.

"I can't believe you're here," Nancy said. "I didn't expect to see you until Friday night."

Eric Campbell smiled. It wasn't a big, flashy,

17

sexy smile, but it sent out signals that always touched something deep inside Nancy and made her shiver. "I had to come into Tarenton to talk to a kid who's entering the program," he said. "I wanted to surprise you."

Eric was a sophomore at the junior college in Hillsborough. When Nancy first met him, he was coaxing a handicapped boy into a swimming pool, gently, calmly telling the boy that there was nothing to be afraid of. Eric wanted to be a physical therapist, and he was the backbone of the college's handicapped students' swimming program. Nancy admired him almost as much as she loved him.

"But how did you know I'd be here?" She gestured toward the other booths at Gino's Pizza. "I almost never come here on a weeknight."

"I got to the high school just as you guys were leaving." Eric smiled again, this time at himself. "So I followed you."

"You're full of surprises," Nancy said softly.

"Talk about surprises!" Angie laughed in delight as she reached for her second slice of pizza. "How did you like Ardith's?"

"I loved it!" Walt said. He jumped up onto the booth beside Olivia and did a modified stag leap. "Freedom! Freedom! Freedom!" Grinning as he sat back down, he asked, "Think we can work up a cheer like that?"

"I think we should just forget about working," Olivia said. She fingered the ends of the immense green and orange muffler. She hadn't taken it off since Walt had ceremoniously wrapped it around

18

her neck. "For five beautiful days, let's enjoy ourselves."

"Good idea," Chris Page said. He picked a mushroom off Angie's slice of pizza and popped it into his mouth. "I'm ready. What's up?"

"A party," Angie said. "Let's have at least one big, terrific party."

All eyes turned to Walt, whose home, a rambling log house with a huge stone fireplace, was perfect for parties.

"Wait a minute," Nancy said. "I'm all for a party, but doesn't anybody else wonder why Ardith gave us time off? I mean, she's never done anything like that before."

"Maybe she's mellowing," Walt suggested. "Finally."

Olivia shook her head. "No. Nancy's right. We haven't been exactly terrific lately, and it's totally out of character for Ardith to let it pass."

"So let's ask her," Walt said.

"No, don't do that!" Angie said quickly. "She might change her mind." She giggled and then said, "Look, why don't we work out a few times on our own? It won't ruin our vacation to practice once or twice. In fact, it might help."

"I'm game." Nancy looked at Eric and smiled. Free time was precious, but she knew Eric would understand if she gave up some of it. He believed that if you wanted something, you worked for it, and he lived by that belief. Nancy wanted the squad to be good. She wanted to please both Ardith and herself, and she was ready to make the effort. "I'll call Mary Ellen and tell her what we think."

19

"Just be careful," Olivia warned. "For two days she's been acting like a volcano that's about to erupt."

"Tell me about it," Nancy said dryly.

Angie leaned forward from the circle of Chris's arm. "Melon's probably just as sick of winter as we are," she said. "Don't worry, she'll be ready to work out with us. She probably already thought of it herself."

The rest of the group eyed Angie fondly. Never a Pollyanna, Angie was always the first to look on the bright side of things. And she detested gossip, which was why she kept quiet when she saw Vanessa Barlow make her entrance into Gino's, followed by Pres Tilford.

"Oh, lovely," Nancy breathed softly when she saw Vanessa. "It's the spider woman."

Vanessa Barlow was tall and dramatically attractive, with thick dark hair and a figure that could only be described with one word — voluptuous. But her appeal was purely physical; there was something beneath that thin veneer of beauty that was sly and calculating and cruel. Ever since failing to make the Varsity Squad, Vanessa had dedicated her life to making its four female members miserable.

"Why does Pres bother with that girl?" Olivia wondered out loud.

"Hormones," Walt said. "Pres is . . . uh . . . at loose ends, lately, so to speak."

"Well, if he's not careful, the spider woman will take permanent care of those loose ends," Nancy commented. "She'll tie them up in her web."

20

"Well, well," Vanessa said as she sidled up to their booth. "It's the Varsity Squad, the former pride of Tarenton High." Her vivid red lips parted in a phony smile. "I say former because, to be perfectly honest, you have been *so* flat lately I was beginning to wonder if you had lead weights in those tacky little skirts you wear."

"Gosh, Vanessa, I must be having ear trouble," Olivia remarked. "I didn't hear anyone ask for your opinion."

Undaunted, Vanessa went on. "I was just telling Pres, as a matter of fact, that what you probably need is some new blood."

Nancy raised her silky dark eyebrows. "If you're volunteering to be a donor, Vanessa, you ought to know that we always check carefully for contamination." She gave a frosty smile. "I'm afraid that rules you out, but thanks, anyway."

Pres shook his head. Alone with Vanessa, he could enjoy her looks and her bristling personality. But when he saw her in action with people he liked, she usually managed to turn him off.

"Come on, Van," he said, and put his hand on the small of her back. "Let's go."

"But I thought you were hungry," Vanessa complained as he steered her away from the booth.

"I am," Pres said. "But not for pizza."

Nancy shook her head as she watched them go. "I'll never understand it."

"I thought you'd understand," Mary Ellen said. "I thought you'd be on my side in this."

"I'm always on your side," Patrick said as he

21

watched her fold her precious letter. "That's why I'm warning you not to get your hopes up too high."

"You must think I'm pretty naive," Mary Ellen fumed. "I'm not some wide-eyed little girl, you know."

"You acted like one in New York."

"That's not fair." Mary Ellen cringed at the memory of her humiliating experience at a New York modeling agency, where she'd been treated like an invisible woman. "This time I have a portfolio. And I've made a commercial. And," she said, jabbing a finger at the letter, "*he* invited *me*!"

Mary Ellen stared glumly out the window of the van. Her little turquoise house shone through the gray day like a neon sign in a run-down neighborhood.

"Hey," Patrick said softly, reaching for her hand. "You're right, you're not a little girl with stars in her eyes." He cupped her chin in his hand and turned her face toward his. "You know I wish you the best."

Mary Ellen's heart melted, but at the same time her thoughts were racing. Maybe he'll actually offer to loan me the money, she thought. Maybe I won't even have to ask.

"But your idea and my idea of 'the best' are different," Patrick continued. "And since your idea doesn't include me, I just can't put a big smile on my face and wave bye-bye when you fly off to Chicago."

"I may not even get to Chicago if — " Mary Ellen stopped herself. She was not going to beg, not from Patrick Henley. But one way or another, she was going to Chicago.

Her jaw squared and her eyes began to sparkle as she considered the future, and Patrick saw the change in her face. He didn't know exactly what she was thinking about, but he would have bet even money her thoughts weren't about him.

Pres turned the Porsche into the drive of his luxurious house on Fable Point, parked the car, and let himself in the back entrance.

His parents weren't home yet. Good. He wouldn't have to make conversation. After exchanging clever, sexy innuendos with Vanessa for the past half hour, he was all talked out. It hadn't even been fun, anyway. Vanessa was good for short stretches, but Pres knew from experience that she tended to fade in the long run. And he was ready for a long run.

He said hello to the maid, grabbed an apple from the fruit basket on the kitchen table, and pounded up the back stairs to his room.

Maybe a little music would help. Since nobody was home, he could use his state-of-the-art stereo system to full advantage. He slipped a tape into the deck, turned the volume up high, and hoped that the beat pounding out of two powerful speakers would drive everything else from his mind.

It didn't work, of course. All it did was make him more restless than ever.

A drive might do it. A quick spin around the lake? The throb of that engine beneath him? It was worth a try.

Pres turned off the tape and at the same instant heard a soft tapping at his door. "Come on in," he called.

The door opened and the maid smiled shyly at him. "I'm sorry to bother you, but I knew you couldn't be asleep, not with all that . . . music."

"Go ahead and call it noise." Pres grinned. "Did somebody complain?"

"No," she said. "You have a phone call. It's long distance, or I wouldn't have disturbed you."

"Thanks." Pres watched her leave and then picked up his bedside phone.

"Hello, Pres?" a female voice said. "This is Blake."

"Blake?"

"Blake Norton." There was a throaty chuckle. "Remember Manhattan?"

CHAPTER

Blake laughed again, and the sound brought Pres's memory alive. He remembered a small, dark-haired girl with striking good looks standing on a windy street corner in New York City. Pres had seen plenty of impressive things when the squad had traveled to the Big Apple to film the Clean Soap commercial, but the most impressive, by far, was Blake Norton. If bold self-reliance could be packaged and sold, Blake would make a killing. She had taken charge of the squad at one of their lowest points — when they'd lost their money and nothing was going right with the commercial. She'd treated them to dinner, shown them the sights, and single-handedly cheered them up. All that for a bunch of strangers. They'd been slightly awed by her at first, but since Blake was so genuinely open and honest, they'd soon counted her as a friend. But Pres's feelings had gone beyond friendship, and now he realized that his memories weren't dead at all — they'd just been buried.

"Sure I remember," he said. "How could I forget?" Pres spoke lightly, but he wasn't really joking. Blake was an exciting girl; if he hadn't been so involved with Claudia when they were making the commercial, something might have developed between them. Trying to sound as if he were used to getting calls from beautiful New York City girls, he asked, "What's up?"

"What's up, huh?" Blake sounded mildly insulted. "I call you out of the blue and all you can ask is, 'What's up?' "

Pres grinned. "Hey, I'm really glad you called," he said, no longer pretending to be blasé. "I'm a little surprised, though. I mean, how long has it been?"

"Long enough, don't you think?"

"Yeah, I do." Pres was beginning to warm up, fast. "What do you think we can do about it?"

"How about if I get on a plane to Tarenton?" Blake suggested.

Pres sat up straight, wondering if he'd heard right. "Are you *serious*?"

"Sure I'm serious," Blake said. "Don't you remember, I told you maybe someday I'd come for a visit and get a taste of the small-town life?"

"I remember. I guess I just thought it was one of those things people say."

"Well, it wasn't," Blake told him. "I've just been waiting for the right time, and it finally came. My parents are going to some psychiatrists' convention in Chicago," she went on. "And since my school's on midyear recess, I'm going with them. Tarenton's on the flight path, so I thought I might stop over for a couple of days, if it's all right with you."

"If it's *all right*?" Pres smiled into the phone. "It's more than all right. It's perfect! When?"

Blake laughed. "Does Saturday sound okay?"

"Well, let's see. This is Thursday," Pres said. "I guess I can wait till Saturday. What time?"

"The plane gets in at noon."

"I'll be there."

Blake laughed again. "You know, I was actually a little afraid to call."

"You? Afraid?"

"Yeah, weird, huh?" Blake said. "I just didn't want to seem pushy, but I guess I didn't have to worry."

"You're right, you didn't," Pres told her softly. "And Blake?"

"Yes?"

"You can push your way into my life anytime."

When Pres hung up, he discovered he was more full of energy than ever. But now there was a difference. Now there was a focus for that energy. What had he been hoping for? A girl in his arms, a little fire in his life? Now he had them, or almost. And the best part was that Blake Norton wasn't just any girl. She'd more than fill his arms, and the fire she'd already started was going to last a long, long time. Pres was sure of it.

"Look," Mary Ellen said grumpily, "I told you I was perfectly willing to do some extra workouts, not that I think it'll help. Just set them up and let me know the time, okay?"

27

"No, it's not okay." Nancy pulled off an over-sized blue cotton-knit sweater and folded it carefully. "You're the squad captain, Mary Ellen. You should be the one calling the shots, not me."

Mary Ellen sighed and stepped into a pair of sweat shorts. "I know I'm the captain, Nancy. But the extra workouts were your idea, so why don't you handle them?" With another sigh, she flopped down on a bench and started pulling on her socks.

Angie and Olivia raised their eyebrows at each other, but Nancy leaned against a locker and peered at Mary Ellen intently. It was Friday, the last day before vacation. They were all getting ready for their final workout with Mrs. Engborg, and Nancy, for one, didn't like Mary Ellen's attitude, which was indifferent, to put it mildly. "Okay," she said finally. "Sunday at ten. In the morning. How's that?"

"Mmm."

"Was that a yes or a no?"

"It was an 'I don't care,'" Mary Ellen told her.

Nancy's patience faded completely. "That's just the problem," she pointed out icily. "If the captain of the squad doesn't care, then why should anybody else?"

"Oh, Nancy, give me a break, will you, please?" Mary Ellen stood up and faced the other girl. "I care and you know it."

"You could have fooled me." Nancy frowned and started to say something withering, something that would shake some spirit into Mary Ellen, but she caught Angie's eye and stopped herself. Angie was shaking her head and looking

28

sympathetic. Nancy didn't really believe that sympathy was going to work any miracles on Mary Ellen, but she decided to give it a try. If sympathy didn't work, *then* she'd get mad. "What's wrong, Mary Ellen?" she asked quietly. "You've been acting like your pet just died or something. Except you don't have a pet," she said with a slight grin, "so that can't be the problem."

"We're not really trying to pry," Olivia said. "We just want to know."

"What is it, Melon?" Angie asked softly. "Maybe we can help."

Mary Ellen slumped back down on the bench. "I guess there's no sense trying to shrug it off, is there? Not with you guys."

"That's right," Nancy said. "We'll get it out of you if we have to hang you upside down from the gym rafters."

Mary Ellen smiled and shook her head. "You don't have to do that. I'll tell you." And she went on to describe her situation in detail, quoting Martin Seltzman's letter almost word for word. "So that's why I've been acting like a . . . a . . . ."

"A witch." Angie touched Mary Ellen's shoulder, taking the sting out of the word.

"Don't be so nice, Angie," Mary Ellen said. "It's just that I feel so frustrated. Sometimes I wish I wanted to be a . . . a painter. At least I could afford the brushes."

The other three were silent for a moment. Nancy and Olivia both knew they could offer Mary Ellen loans. But they also knew she'd never accept them. Angie had the same financial problems as Mary Ellen, so she was stuck just feeling

29

bad for her friend and wishing she could think of some way to cheer her up.

"Look," she said positively, "someday when you're a famous model, Martin Seltzman will probably be sending a limousine to pick you up from your Park Avenue penthouse. In the meantime. . . ."

"In the meantime, shape up," Nancy finished. But she was smiling to show she understood what Mary Ellen was going through.

"You're right, I know," Mary Ellen agreed. "I've got to stop feeling sorry for myself. It's a disgusting habit to get into."

"Everyone's entitled to a little self-pity once in a while," Olivia said. "Besides, there are worse habits. You could be a compulsive gambler. Or eater. Or," she said, lowering her voice dramatically, "you could drink. Then we'd have to kick you off the squad. For self-pity, you get a second chance."

"Okay, okay, I get the picture," Mary Ellen laughed. "You guys forgive me, right?"

"Sure we do," Nancy said. "Of course, you're on probation, you realize. One more slipup and you're in big trouble."

"There won't be any more slipups," Mary Ellen said. "Promise. Thanks, you guys. And Sunday's fine with me. Let's just make it for two o'clock. Nobody'll have even one eye open at ten."

"You're the captain." Olivia prodded Mary Ellen in the back. "Come on, Ardith's been waiting so long she's probably mad enough to spit nails. Lead on!"

"Tarenton, Tarenton,
You've got the knack!
They're on the run
So don't hold back!"

If good intentions counted for anything, the cheer would have been terrific. Technically, it was sharp and clean, but like all the routines the squad had been doing lately, it was missing the "oomph," as Ardith called it, that could make it sparkle.

Mary Ellen had been sure that her talk with Nancy, Olivia, and Angie had cleared her mind, but when it came down to it, she realized her smile was insincere and as brittle as cold toast. And even though her body seemed in sync, her mind kept wandering. She decided to blame Vanessa Barlow, who was lurking in the bleachers with her latest man, a hunk of a guy whose brain could probably fit into his little toe. Mary Ellen knew she couldn't really blame Vanessa for her poor performance, but she was an easy target. Easier than facing the fact that she hadn't stopped feeling sorry for herself.

Walt, Olivia, Angie, and Nancy also tried hard, but if they'd been given a truth serum they would have confessed that their minds just weren't on cheerleading. They were already looking ahead to a week of almost complete freedom.

Of all of them, Pres had the most energy. That was his problem. The thoughts of Blake Norton had him so wired that the others were scrambling just to keep up with him.

The cheer ended and Ardith put her chin in her hands. It was tempting, very tempting, to chew out the squad quite royally. But she'd already decided to let the cheerleaders stew in their own juices, and she was determined she'd stick to that decision. "All right," she said crisply. "One more time, and then we'll call it quits."

Quickly, wanting to get the practice over with, the squad reassembled and started the cheer. On the word *knack*, Olivia was supposed to start a series of back handsprings that would take her to the center of the floor, where Pres was waiting to lift her to his shoulders. She began the handsprings, her small, compact body whirling with no visible effort, then landed on her feet. Arms outstretched, body poised, she waited to feel Pres's hands on her waist.

Two seconds passed. No hands. Olivia saw the others beginning the cartwheels that would bring *them* to the center of the floor, and still no Pres. She glanced around. Pres hadn't moved. He was staring at the floor, his mouth hanging open like a puppy's. Annoyed, Olivia looked to see what had distracted him.

Blake Norton was standing in the doorway. By the time Olivia had registered that fact, the rest of the squad had noticed Pres's catatonic state and had also looked toward the source of it. They all recognized the dark-haired girl at once, and instead of ending with *back!* the cheer ended, resoundingly, with the word *Blake!* The formation broke up, and the squad streaked over to greet their friend from New York.

"This is incredible!" Angie squealed. "What are you doing here?"

"Just passing through," Blake told them in her low, husky voice. "Didn't Pres mention it?"

Pres, who had recovered enough to talk, stepped in close to Blake and put his hand on her shoulder. "I was going to tell them today," he said. "Since I didn't expect you till tomorrow, I thought I had plenty of time. Not that I mind, but why are you here early?"

"Oh, you know me, I never do anything by the book." Blake laughed, delighted with her surprise. "Actually, my parents took an earlier plane, so I jumped in a cab when I got to Tarenton. Not that a cab was that easy to come by. I figured I'd find you guys here."

"You look fabulous," Mary Ellen said, feeling distinctly disheveled and sweaty beside Blake's laid-back sophistication. She was wearing black jersey stirrup pants tucked into tangerine-colored ankle-high boots. To top it off, she wore an enormous loose-knit sweater striped in every color of the rainbow. She would have looked like the Cheshire cat except that her grin was too fresh and honest to be conniving.

Vanessa had also been studying Blake, and decided she was getting too much attention. Eyeing Blake's outfit with distaste, she clicked her tongue. "Is that what they're wearing in New York these days?"

"Oh, Vanessa!" Blake's tone carried just a hint of contempt. "I didn't expect to find you in enemy territory. You're either brave or masochistic."

"She's both," Walt said, and everyone laughed.

"Blake?" Ardith held out her hand and Blake shook it. "It's nice to see you again."

"Thanks. Same to you, Mrs. Engborg. Listen," Blake said quickly, "I didn't mean to interrupt anything here. I'll just take a seat and you go ahead with what you were doing."

"Well, thank you, but I think we've all had just about enough of what we were doing." Ardith gave the squad a brittle smile. "I have to talk to Superintendent Barlow for a few minutes. See you at the game tomorrow night."

Ardith left, followed by Vanessa and her hunk, and the squad quickly forgot the fact that they hadn't even finished the workout. They crowded around Blake, asking questions, sharing news, and suggesting things they'd do while she was in town.

Only Pres stood back from the fray. From the moment he'd seen Blake standing in the open door of the gym, one hand on her hip, he'd felt himself falling further and further in love. It was all he could do to keep what his father would call "an imbecilic grin" under control. He'd look away from Blake and consciously straighten his lips; then he'd glance at her, see a gold loop earring brush against the curve of her cheek, watch her wind a short black curl around her finger, and he'd feel his mouth lift helplessly in a foolish smile.

Foolishness and helplessness were alien feelings for Pres. That was why he stood apart from the group, not because he didn't want to be close to Blake. It was the desire to be close that made him stand back — he was afraid to be so emotionally naked in front of the others. But at the first break in the conversation, Pres stepped in. Putting a hand on the back of Blake's neck, he leaned close to her ear and said, "Hey, I know about airline food. I'll bet you're hungry."

"Ravenous." Blake turned her dark eyes on him and Pres nearly melted. "What did you have in mind?" she asked.

Pres took her wrist in a warm grasp and with a silent wave to the rest of the squad, pulled her out into the hallway. "This," he said, and took her in his arms. He'd waited long enough.

CHAPTER

The kiss lasted a long time. Blake finally broke it, pulled back, and looked Pres in the eye. "Well," she said, "hello to you, too!"

Pres laughed and reached for her canvas duffle bag. "Come on, let's get out of here."

As they walked through the parking lot, Blake said, "By the way, I didn't make any reservations. I just figured a motel in Tarenton wouldn't be jammed."

"Motel?" Pres shook his head. "You're staying at my place. My father's on a business trip, but my mother's home and she insisted that you be our guest." He stopped in front of his car. "This is it."

"A Porsche?" Blake raised her eyebrows as she got into the sleek red car. "Don't get me wrong, but I never thought I'd see one of these in Tarenton."

"If it weren't for me, you wouldn't," Pres said.

"This is the one and only. Like it?"

"Sure, what's not to like?" Blake leaned back as the car sped along the lake drive. "It's cleaner than the subway, I'll admit that. Of course, if I were into conspicuous consumption, I'd have bought a Jag."

"Uh oh." Pres looked uncomfortable. "You're not a reverse snob, I hope. Somebody who hates money."

"Me? No way." Blake laughed. "Money's great. Why?"

"Because I've had a lot of that," Pres told her, and pulled the Porsche to a stop in front of his fabulous home.

Blake knew her share of wealthy people so she wasn't ruffled by the Tilfords' financial status. She did find the wealth revealing, though. It explained a lot about Pres — the way he carried himself, his smooth manners, his assurance, and even his name. Preston was definitely a rich kid's name.

The money didn't explain why he was a cheerleader, however, which was something Blake was extremely curious about. It didn't seem like a very cool thing to do, and Pres was nothing if not cool. Once he introduced her to his mother, however, the answers started clicking into place. Felicia Tilford was beautiful and pleasant, but so reserved that Blake half expected her to fade into the silk wallpaper of her formal dining room.

"Pres told me you're from New York City, Blake," Mrs. Tilford said, smiling. "I'll never forget the time Mr. Tilford and I were there. We saw *Aida* at the Met. It was wonderful."

Blake swallowed a spoonful of raspberry sherbet and nodded. "I'll bet you stayed at the Plaza," she said, mentioning one of Manhattan's most expensive hotels.

"Why, yes, we did." Mrs. Tilford sighed. "What a lovely place that is." She subtly signaled for the maid to clear the table. "Pres mentioned that you attend Dunwood Academy. I had a college friend who went there. I often wish Tarenton had the same kind of high-quality private school."

"Tarenton High's one of the best in the state, you know, Mom," Pres reminded her.

"Oh, yes, I realize that. But Dunwood Academy. . . ." She shook her head wistfully and didn't finish the sentence.

Blake gave Pres a conspiratorial wink across the immense, glossy dining table, and later, when they were alone, she said, "I get it now. You don't really like being a cheerleader. You just did it to get a reaction."

Pres laughed. "That's partly right. I have to admit, I really enjoyed the look on my parents' faces when I told them. I mean, Preston Tilford III a *cheerleader*?" He smiled at the memory. "But now it's not like that at all. Now I love it."

Blake looked unconvinced.

"I do," Pres insisted. "You know, Blake Norton, in some ways you're as big a snob as my folks. You wait until you see the squad in action tomorrow night. Then tell me you think cheerleading is a weird thing for a guy to do."

"Okay, okay. Never let it be said that I have a closed mind." Blake shouldered her duffle bag and followed Pres up the stairs to the guest room.

"Actually, I'm looking forward to seeing you guys in action. I saw the commercial, but I'm sure it's not the same thing as seeing you in the flesh — no pun intended."

"No comment," Pres said with a grin. He stopped outside one of the guest room doors and then he put his arms around her for the second time that day. "I still can't believe you're here," he whispered, his lips against her hair.

"Believe it," Blake told him. She lifted her head and met his lips with hers. It was a wonderful kiss, and she thoroughly enjoyed it until she happened to catch a glimpse of Pres's eyes as he pulled back. There was a look in them that bothered her. What was it? Possessive? Self-satisfied? She couldn't put her finger on his expression, but whatever it said, she didn't like the message.

She saw the look again the next day and she still didn't like it. But she decided to ignore it until she could figure out why she felt so troubled.

"Okay," she said at breakfast, "I'm ready."

"Ready for what?" Pres asked.

"Ready to discover the charms of Tarenton. I showed you my town, now you show me yours."

"You didn't really come to see Tarenton, I hope."

"Sure I did. What'd you think?"

Pres frowned slightly. "Well, I sort of thought you came here to see me."

"That, too," Blake laughed. "You and Walt and Angie and Nancy and Olivia and Mary Ellen. Oh. And Patrick."

At the mention of Patrick's name, Pres spilled his orange juice. "I almost forgot!" he said, mopping up the puddle with a napkin. "Patrick and I have a job in — " he checked his watch " — in half an hour."

"A job? I didn't know you worked," Blake said.

"I'm rich but I'm not lazy," Pres joked. "Patrick and I are in the moving business together," he explained. "That ticked my folks off, too, but they can't gripe much, since Patrick and I are really making a go of it."

"Well, well, I'm impressed," Blake said. "I'm more impressed with that than with your Porsche."

"Thanks." Pres moved behind her chair and put his hands on her shoulders. "The only problem is, I can't get out of the job this morning. It's too late."

"Why should you get out of it?"

"So I can be with you," Pres whispered in her ear. "Now you'll be stuck here without me."

"Stuck? In the house? No way!" Blake stood up and held out her hand. "Give me the keys to your car."

"To the Porsche?"

"Sure. Unless you've got another one stashed away somewhere." Blake laughed at the look on Pres's face. "Come on, I'm a good driver. I won't put a single scratch on that baby of yours."

Pres agreed, and half an hour later, when Patrick came by in the van, Blake was just peeling off in the Porsche. As she neared the end of the private drive, she stuck a hand out the window and waved.

Pres laughed. "Isn't she something?"

Patrick nodded and looked at his friend. Pres was showing all the symptoms of having been bitten by the love bug — a dreamy look in the eyes, silly smiles that came and went for no apparent reason, a barely audible hum under his breath. Patrick had been hoping to have a serious discussion about Mary Ellen. But with Pres walking two feet off the ground, they'd be lucky to simply get the moving job done.

"Come on," he said, giving Pres a nudge. "Let's get to work. The faster we move that office furniture, the faster you can get back to Blake."

On the other side of town, Mary Ellen was trying to force herself to get up and get moving. Moving for what, she didn't know, but she'd made a pact with herself to forget Chicago and get on with her life. Well, maybe not *forget*, exactly. She knew she'd never be able to do that. But if she couldn't have it, well, there were plenty of other things she could have. Breakfast, for starters.

She pushed back the covers and hopped out of bed. The bedroom she shared with her little sister, Gemma, was chilly, and she reached quickly for her dusty-rose-colored terrycloth bathrobe.

"Psst. Mary Ellen." Gemma's sleepy eyes peeped over the edge of her blanket. "Don't use up all the hot water, okay? And turn the heat up before you shower. And let's have cocoa for breakfast."

41

"I suppose you'd like a hot water bottle and a tray in bed, too," Mary Ellen said, pulling on her slipper socks.

"That sounds great!"

"Doesn't it?" Mary Ellen tossed her pillow at Gemma and laughed. "Why don't you just ring for the maid?"

Still laughing, she padded out into the hall and headed for the bathroom, shivering. The house was icy, but as she passed the living room she heard the familiar click of the thermostat and felt the floor shudder as the furnace came on. She stopped at the living room door. "Dad?"

"Hi, honey." Mr. Kirkwood nudged the thermostat up another notch, frowning, and chivied it back down. He was wearing his bus driver's uniform.

"I didn't know you had to work this morning," Mary Ellen said. Usually, her father worked Saturday afternoons.

"Wish I didn't." Mr. Kirkwood gave the thermostat one last worried glance before moving away from it. "It's this weather, sweetheart. It just won't warm up and our heating bills have been sky-high. I'm taking on a few extra shifts, otherwise we'll get so far behind in our payments we'll never see daylight." He picked up his lunchbox and zipped his jacket. "See you at dinner?"

"I don't think so," Mary Ellen said. "There's a game tonight."

"Well, then, see you at breakfast tomorrow." He gave his daughter a distracted kiss on the cheek and strode quickly toward the front door.

Mary Ellen stood for a moment in the living

room, feeling the floor vibrate as the furnace sent warm air through the vents. If her father could work overtime just to help with the heating bills, why couldn't she work overtime and get herself to Chicago? And why hadn't she thought of it before? Else Gunderson, the owner of Marnie's, the boutique where Mary Ellen worked, had been a model once. She'd understand better than anyone else just how much getting this break would mean to Mary Ellen. And she might be persuaded to pay her in advance and let Mary Ellen make it up in extra work when she got back from Chicago.

Things weren't over yet! She still had a chance. As Mary Ellen hurried down the hall to shower, her blue eyes were glinting with determination.

"Isn't that Pres's car?" Nancy asked.

"Yes, but that's not Pres at the wheel," Angie said. "It's Blake."

"My gosh," Nancy commented. "Pres must be sitting in the palm of her hands if he actually let her drive his car."

The two cheerleaders stopped outside the entrance to Pineland Mall and watched as Blake expertly threaded the Porsche into a tight parking spot. When Blake got out, she noticed them, waved, and walked over.

"Hi! Pres had to work so I've been exploring your town," she explained. "It's not a bad place to visit."

"But you wouldn't want to live here?" Nancy asked with a laugh.

"I might consider it, in about twenty years."

Blake surveyed the mall. "I'm ravenous," she announced. "Let's find someplace to eat."

"Great idea," Angie agreed quickly. "But I'm afraid you won't find anything very exotic in here."

Nancy nodded. "Definitely no Thai food."

Blake stopped and looked at them. "Hey, you two, don't apologize. I'm having a great time so far."

"I guess we're afraid you'll be bored," Angie admitted.

"Me? Never." Blake grinned. "But I might be dead if I don't get some food in me quick. Come on, let's eat!"

From her "perch," a small raised platform outside Marnie's, Mary Ellen spotted Nancy, Angie, and Blake strolling through the mall together. All three wore legwarmers in vivid shades of red, yellow, and purple. All three were laughing.

"Mary Ellen, hi!" Angie kicked up a yellow-swathed leg. "Look what Blake dug up," she said, pointing to her legwarmers.

"Dug up is right," Nancy said. "She found them in this little hole-in-the-wall shop no one under thirty ever goes into. I think the owner was surprised she had them in stock."

"Which is why she gave us such a good buy," Blake said. "Keep quiet about it or the prices'll go up."

"Guess what?" Angie's blue eyes widened in amazement. "Pres let Blake drive his Porsche. Can you believe it?"

"She obviously has him wrapped around her little finger," Nancy said, grinning.

"Please." Blake's mouth puckered as if she'd tasted a lemon. "That's the last thing I need."

Mary Ellen looked at her curiously. She'd just assumed that Blake had traveled to Tarenton because she was as mad about Pres as he was about her. But the thought of having Pres wrapped around her finger was making Blake extremely jittery, and Mary Ellen began to wonder just how much in love Blake was — or if she was in love at all.

She didn't wonder for long, though. She was having enough trouble keeping a smile on her face so no one would suspect that her last hope had just been crushed. Else Gunderson, former model and owner of Marnie's, had been impressed by the letter from the Futura Modeling Agency. And she'd been sympathetic about Mary Ellen's money problem. She'd been encouraging and supportive and kind. She'd been everything except a help. Business had been terrible, Else had explained sadly. She wasn't even sure that she could keep Mary Ellen on the payroll much longer, let alone advance her money against a job that might not exist in the near future.

Mary Ellen had just about decided that her future held only bleakness. But as soon as her friends came up, she quickly tried to compose her face and act interested in their new legwarmers. After all, she'd promised them that she wasn't going to mope anymore. Moping was for losers, and she hadn't quite reached the point where she thought of herself as a loser. Not yet.

"Hey," she said suddenly. "What are you guys doing hanging around the mall, anyway? We've got a game tonight." If she couldn't control her distant future, at least she still had some say in what went on in the next few hours. She was captain of the Varsity Squad, after all. "We've been awful lately, but we can't afford to be bad tonight. We've got this hip New Yorker in the audience, remember?"

"Right," Blake agreed. "I didn't come all the way to Tarenton to see a half-baked performance, you know. I came to be dazzled."

Mary Ellen clapped her hands and grinned at Nancy and Angie. "This is your captain speaking. Go home and rest. Don't stuff yourselves at dinner, either, or you'll be as sluggish as reptiles. Blake want dazzle, and dazzle is what we're going to give her."

Later that night, the Tarenton High gym was packed with spectators from both Tarenton and Hillsborough. It didn't matter that the weather was not cooperating, drenching the streets in wet, freezing snow. Both schools had enthusiastic fans who didn't mind getting their feet wet, or sweating in a crowded gym. They were there to root for their teams, and they didn't root quietly.

Blake sat in the bleachers with Patrick Henley, following the game intently. Patrick seemed surprised by her enthusiasm. "I guess I didn't expect you to get so caught up in something like this," he said, when Blake had loudly booed a referee for a call against Tarenton. "I thought New Yorkers were too cool for that."

"Are you kidding?" Blake shouted over the roar of the crowd. "I'm a rabid Knicks' fan. I

46

guess some New Yorkers think going crazy over a basketball team is beneath them," she admitted. "Mostly the ones I go to school with." Blake barely tolerated the snobbish environment of Dunwood Academy, the posh private school her parents insisted she attend. "But I love this stuff. All right!" she shouted, as a Tarenton player streaked across the floor to Hillsborough's basket. "Sink it!"

On the sidelines, the Varsity Squad was just going into the "Don't Hold Back" cheer, and Blake watched, impressed, as the six cheerleaders went through a twisting, gyrating routine that was half dance and half gymnastics. It ended with Pres and Walt doing stag leaps, and when Pres landed, he raised his eyes to Blake and grinned.

Patrick saw Pres's face and grinned, too. "I guess I don't have to tell you that Pres has been higher than a kite ever since you arrived."

"You're right," Blake agreed. "You don't have to tell me." "Don't Hold Back" seemed like the perfect cheer for Pres to be doing at the moment. Ever since he'd pulled Blake out of the gym and into his arms the day before, he'd been holding himself back — but just barely.

> "Tarenton, Tarenton,
> You're right on track,
> You're number one!
> Don't hold back!"

As the cheer ended, Pres's eyes sought out Blake again. There was no question as to who was number one for *him*. His feelings were right

47

on the surface, and Blake didn't have any trouble reading them. Pres wanted her. She could feel it in his arms and lips, and see it in his eyes. He was about as subtle as a bulldozer, and Blake knew that if she didn't do something fast, she was going to get plowed under by all that emotion.

CHAPTER 5

Pres took his eyes off the road and glanced over at Blake. It was times like these when he wished the Porsche was just a plain old sedan, with a single front seat instead of two buckets. Then the stick shift wouldn't be in the way, and Blake could scoot over next to him. He wanted her as close to him as possible. He wanted to feel his arm brush hers, and maybe put his hand on the back of her neck. He loved her neck, especially where the black curls met the white skin.

He glanced at her again and almost laughed aloud at himself. Even if Blake wasn't wearing a seat belt, even if there were no stick shift between them, he could probably never persuade her to slide closer to him. She wasn't the type to cuddle in a car. What type she was, he wasn't sure. She was smart and sexy and honest to the point of being blunt. But she had a soft side, too. Not soft-weak — soft-sensitive. She tried to hide it, but it came through, no matter how many layers of East Coast veneer she used to cover it. Pres decided it was precisely this combination of boldness and softness that turned him on. Really turned him on.

"Tell me," he said with a grin, "what do you think of cheerleading now?" When he'd first told Blake he was a cheerleader, she'd almost fallen off her high-heeled boots.

"You guys were terrific! I mean, I saw the commercial, but I've always liked live action better," Blake said. "And this was live, all right."

Pres's smile got wider. "You should see us when we're really on."

"You mean you weren't?"

"Well, we were better than we've been in a week, but we're still not up to par," Pres explained. "I think we were good tonight because you were there. Keep on coming and we'll really show you what 'live' is all about."

Blake made a face. "No thanks. You guys'll have to get it together on your own. I'm not about to be anybody's mascot."

Pres threw back his head and laughed. "I didn't mean you should be a mascot. I meant you were an inspiration." He reached out and took her hand. "It was a compliment."

"Yeah?" Blake frowned and stared at their hands. "I'm not sure I want to be an inspiration, either."

"Why not?" Pres asked as he pulled the car to a stop in front of his home. "Anyway, you don't have a choice. You already inspire me."

"Inspire you to what?" Blake asked curiously.

"To this." Sliding over as far as the gear shift allowed, Pres put his arms around Blake and smiled into her dark eyes. He traced her beautiful red lips with a finger and then kissed her. The kiss started out softly, but it grew more intense. "You're so fantastic, Blake," he murmured. "I never want to let go of you."

"Yeah, well, if you don't," Blake said in a matter-of-fact tone of voice, "I'm going to rip this gear shift out. It's poking me in the thigh and it's killing me."

Instead of feeling insulted, Pres felt more attracted to Blake than ever. "You're fantastic!" he exclaimed, shaking his head and laughing.

"You already said that," Blake reminded him, reaching for the door handle. "Not that I mind being told, but I guess a Porsche just isn't the best place for passion."

As they walked toward the front door, Pres caught her hand. "Hey, Blake, I didn't mean to come on so strong." Pres meant what he said, but just the touch of her hand made him want to put his arms around her. "I just can't get over your being here." He did put his arms around her, sighing deeply. "I know this is going to sound crazy, but I think I'm in — "

"You want to know what's crazy?" Blake interrupted quickly. "Standing out here freezing when we could be inside your warm mansion." She slipped her arm through his and pulled him toward the door. "Besides, you're giving a party tonight, remember?"

Pres let himself be pulled, but he couldn't help wishing he'd never decided to throw a party.

51

True, it was supposed to be a kickoff for the mid-year recess, and Blake was the guest of honor. But if he hadn't opened his big mouth and invited the entire squad, he might have had Blake all to himself tonight.

As the party got going, though, Pres got into the swing of it and enjoyed himself. For one thing, his family room, an immense space with a view of the lake, wasn't as rigidly formal as other rooms in the Tilford house. The oriental rugs, with their intricate red, beige, and blue designs, added warmth and color to the polished hardwood floors. The couches were soft and deep, and best of all, there was plenty of room for dancing.

Then there was the food. Pres was no slouch when it came to goodies, and besides a three-foot hero, there were enough cheese, crackers, dips, and sandwich-makings to last a week.

The company was terrific, too. Even though the cheerleaders hadn't been meshing in their routines lately, personally they were getting along great. In fact, Pres was in such a good mood that he felt like kissing every one of them. The only fly in the ointment was Vanessa Barlow, who had come because she had a date with one of the basketball players Pres had invited.

But Pres didn't really see Vanessa, much as she tried to put herself in his line of vision. He didn't see her, and he barely noticed anyone else. Blake was there, and for Pres, Blake was the only one really worth looking at.

"He's like a little kid," Nancy observed from her vantage point near the window overlooking the lake. "He can't keep his eyes off her."

"Eyes?" Walt reached for another slice of hero and chuckled. "Look at his hands. The minute she gets out of reach, his hands start twitching. He's got it bad!"

"So what?" Olivia asked. "Blake's great. Why shouldn't Pres have it bad for her?"

"I agree." Nancy tightened her grip on Eric Campbell's hand. "When you find someone who's great for you, that's not the time to hold back."

"You should go for it, you mean?" Chris Page asked.

"I didn't mean that in a . . . a physical way," Nancy claimed. "I just meant that if you're in love, there's no sense in trying to hide from it."

Chris rubbed the back of Angie's neck and smiled. "That's what I meant, too."

"Well, now that we all agree," Walt said, "let's dance."

He took Olivia's small hand in his big one, and the two of them stood up and began to move to the music.

Chris kept his arm around Angie, who was staring off into space not saying much. "Feel like dancing, too?" he asked.

Angie nodded. "I'd better do something to work off all that dip I've eaten," she said. But she didn't move, and when Pres and Blake went dancing by, Angie frowned.

"What is it, Ange?" Nancy asked.

"I'm not sure," Angie said with a slight shake of her head. "It's just that we've been talking about how hard Pres has fallen for Blake. I was wondering if Blake feels the same way."

"She has to feel something," Nancy pointed out. "She came all the way to Tarenton to see him."

"I know," Angie agreed. "I'm sure she cares about him. But Blake's so . . . you know, so independent. I don't think she's ready to get tied down."

"Well, who said anything about tying her down?" Nancy asked.

"Nobody," Angie said. Then she giggled. "But look at Pres. If the rest of us weren't here, he'd probably be proposing marriage."

They all looked at the dark blond cheerleader dancing with Blake Norton. Angie was right. Pres's handsome face was an open book, and if he wasn't careful, his heart was going to fall off his sleeve and get stepped on — hard.

Blake's face wasn't so easy to read. She looked spectacular in the same black pants topped, this time, with a big-cut paisley blouse. She smiled a lot and laughed a lot, and made everyone else laugh a lot with her stories of the New York scene. Only Vanessa didn't appreciate Blake's presence, because Blake definitely outclassed her. But since only Vanessa's date paid any attention to her, Vanessa's irritation didn't really matter.

Blake's face didn't give a clue as to what she was feeling, and Blake wasn't about to tell anyone. Angie had been close when she called it "tied-down." But smothered was more like it. Blake felt smothered — by Pres, of all people. By Pres's smiles, his kisses, his touch, his attention. Now, Pres was one great guy. A prince, she'd called him after they'd gotten to know each other in New York.

He was still a prince, and Blake knew that. But now he was acting like a prince on a big white horse, ready to swoop her up and carry her off to his castle. Blake didn't want to be swooped up, whether it was onto a horse or into a Porsche. And as for his castle, she was already in it. Big as it was, she still felt smothered. It had definitely been a mistake not to stay in a motel.

The music ended and Pres immediately grabbed her hand. "Come help me pick out some more records, okay?"

"Hey, I think I'll let you handle that," Blake told him. "I need a Coke." And before Pres could offer to get it for her, which she was sure he would, Blake walked through the crowd of laughing kids and headed for the butler's pantry.

The pantry was a room devoted almost entirely to the storage of Felica Tilford's finest china and linen. It was dark, it was quiet, and it was private, which was why Mary Ellen and Patrick were having an argument there.

It had been Patrick's idea to retreat to the privacy of the pantry, and when Mary Ellen agreed, she'd felt that she now understood the meaning of the term *gold digger*. She just couldn't keep from hoping that Patrick was going to offer to loan her the money to go to Chicago. In her eyes that made herself a gold digger, and she felt guilty about it. But the guilt didn't stop her from hoping.

Patrick, however, had something else on his

mind. Kissing, to be exact. "I just had to tell you," he whispered when they were alone, "how fabulous you look tonight. You're beautiful, Mary Ellen. Really beautiful."

"Oh, Patrick." With his arms around her, Mary Ellen always had trouble focusing on anything. She lifted her head and kissed him without even bothering to tell herself that it could never last.

When the kiss was over, Patrick kept holding her. "I know how unhappy you've been about that modeling interview," he said softly. "It must have meant a lot to you."

Meant? Mary Ellen stiffened in his arms. What did he mean, "meant"? Pulling back, she stared at his face. Content was the only word for the way Patrick looked at the moment, and Mary Ellen didn't like that look one bit. "I don't think you know how much it *means* to me," she told him. "If you did, you wouldn't talk about the interview in the past tense, like it's over and done with."

"But it is over and done with, right?" Patrick asked.

"You'd like it to be, wouldn't you?" Mary Ellen pulled completely away from him and leaned against one of the glass-fronted china cabinets. "You'd like it if I'd never even gotten that letter. What you'd really like is for me not to have a single goal in my life except to please you. If we were married, you'd want me barefoot and pregnant. And in the kitchen!"

"That's not fair," Patrick stated heatedly. "You know it's not. You know I care about what you want."

"Sure you do, just as long as it doesn't interfere

56

with what *you* want." Mary Ellen knew she wasn't being fair, but all the hurt and disappointment about Chicago were finally spilling out, and she couldn't stop the flood. "That modeling interview isn't dead and buried, Patrick. It still means a lot to me. And even if I have to hitchhike, I'm going to Chicago!"

At that moment, Blake made her escape into the butler's pantry. She took one look at Mary Ellen and Patrick, and did a quick about-face. "Sorry," she said, quickly heading for the door. "Just pretend I was never here."

"Don't go, Blake," Patrick called after her.

"No," Blake said over her shoulder. "You guys don't need my company."

"Wrong." Patrick caught up with and passed her. "It's each other's company we don't need," he said, nodding in Mary Ellen's direction. With that, he strode out the door.

Blake turned and eyed Mary Ellen in the semi-dark room. "Sorry about that," she said. "I really didn't mean to interrupt anything."

"Don't apologize," Mary Ellen told her in a shaky voice. "Patrick was right. If we'd stayed here much longer we would have been at each other's throats."

Mary Ellen was obviously much more upset than she was letting on, but Blake wasn't inclined to pry. Still, it didn't seem right to just walk off and leave her alone when she was so down. She went over and leaned against the cabinet, next to Mary Ellen.

The girls stared at each other's reflections in the glass-fronted cabinet that stood opposite them, and then Blake cleared her throat. "So," she commented, "you're thumbing your way to Chicago, huh?"

Mary Ellen shook her head and managed a wry smile. "No, but if I weren't such a coward, I'd be out on the highway right now."

"Yeah?" Blake looked at her curiously. "What's in Chicago besides the psychiatrists' convention my parents are going to?"

"The Futura Modeling Agency," Mary Ellen said immediately.

"Huh?"

Without going into great detail, Mary Ellen told Blake the story. When she finished, she thought of something that made her smile again. "Hey, you're going to Chicago. Want to get into modeling? I've got a contact there."

Blake snorted. "Hah. Put me in front of a camera and I'm an instant klutz. No, I've got it," she chuckled. "You go to Chicago for me. You can have your interview and stand in for me with my parents."

"I'd do it in a second," Mary Ellen grinned, "but I don't think your folks would appreciate the switch."

"Are you kidding?" Blake asked. "They'd be so happy to get somebody like you for a daughter, they'd probably never let you go."

"Come on, I can't believe that."

"Yeah, well, maybe not." Blake shrugged.

"Anyway," Mary Ellen went on, "if we traded places, then you'd have to be varsity captain."

"Oh, I forgot about that." Blake rolled her

eyes in mock horror. "I don't think the squad would survive me. Or I wouldn't survive the squad. Anyway, it would mean the end for both of us."

"Well, it was a nice idea, anyway." Mary Ellen laughed and realized she felt much better. Blake had commiserated with her, but not in a way that made Mary Ellen feel sorry for herself or get all weepy. "I'm glad you came in here," she told Blake. "You cheered me up."

"Yeah, well, if we can't trade places, at least we can stick together," Blake said. "Come on, let's get back to the others. If I don't show up in another minute, Pres'll probably organize a search party." She paused at the door, cocked her head, and looked at Mary Ellen. "Does he always come on this strong?"

"Well. . . ." Mary Ellen thought about it. She'd had her own flings with Pres, but they'd never led to anything because of Patrick. "I don't really know how it feels to have him crazy about me, like he is about you," she admitted. "He's not shy, that's for sure."

"Tell me about it."

"It's been a while since Pres had a girl friend," Mary Ellen said with a grin.

Blake pursed her lips and nodded. "That's what I was afraid of."

Later, after the party was over and everyone had gone, Blake lay awake in her guest-room bed, in the opposite wing of the house from Pres's room. She couldn't sleep, but it didn't bother her. She was a night person, anyway.

What bothered her were her thoughts. She had until Friday before she was supposed to leave and join her parents in Chicago, and she didn't know if she could handle Pres for another hour, let alone another four days.

CHAPTER

Sunday was the first clear day Tarenton had had in over a week. The weatherman had promised more clouds on Monday, but nobody was looking that far ahead. After nine days of snow and drizzle and sleet, everyone was ready to live for the moment.

Sunday was also the first day of freedom for Tarenton High's Varsity Cheerleading Squad. And the moment *they* were living was the workout they'd scheduled at two that afternoon.

The gym, which the group had gotten permission to use, reverberated with the throbbing beat of rock music from Olivia's portable cassette deck as the six cheerleaders went through their various limbering-up exercises. Nobody was really in the mood to be there, but nobody wanted to admit it, either. So the bending and stretching went on in near silence, without the quips and jokes that were usually passed around.

Nancy, her dark hair tied back with a piece of crimson yarn, did a slow backbend and wondered how Eric was doing. She knew what he was doing — he was coaching Jimmy Michaels, a ten-year-old who'd spent almost a year in a wheelchair and now needed a lot of therapy to regain his muscle tone. Nancy had been making good progress with Jimmy. The progress, and the shy smile he always gave her, made her volunteer work especially rewarding.

Sundays she usually worked with Jimmy. But with the squad's workout, she'd had to turn the job over to Eric, and she felt guilty.

"Don't worry about it," Eric had said when she'd told him. "I have to be there, anyway."

"I know," Nancy said. "But I feel like I'm letting you down. And Jimmy, too."

"Well, Jimmy's going to feel let down, that's for sure," Eric teased. "I'm not nearly as pretty as you are."

Eric took his commitments so seriously that Nancy was relieved he'd let her off the hook with a joke. But she still felt guilty, and as she rested a moment and watched Angie do her leg stretches, she promised herself that she'd put in some extra time this week to make it up to him. And to Jimmy.

Angie rubbed her hands on her faded pink sweat pants and tried to banish Christopher Page from her mind, at least for an hour or so. It wasn't easy, especially on a rare, clear day like this. Chris was at the library, waiting for her. And next to the library was a park, with a pond and winding walks and secluded benches. If she hadn't been so gung ho as to suggest the squad work out on its own, she could have been sitting on one of those secluded benches with Chris.

Get with it, Angie, she told herself. No pain, no gain. Then she started stretching again, hoping she'd have some energy left over for Chris.

Neither Walt nor Olivia was feeling guilty about not wanting to be in the gym on such a bright day. Then again, they hadn't been able to agree on where they would have gone. It was nothing important — just one of those minor arguments that kept cropping up.

Olivia, who looked at a physical challenge the way a bull looks at a red cape, had been all for taking up cross-country skiing, while there was still enough snow.

Walt, who sometimes wished that Olivia was just a little less energetic, had had visions of their spending the free time in front of a roaring fire, talking, kissing, and eating popcorn, depending on which appetite moved them at the moment.

Since they hadn't been able to agree, they'd both figured they might as well attend the workout. But they went through their warm-up paces mechanically, with about as much conviction as puppets.

"Okay, troops," Mary Ellen called. She turned off the music and tried to pretend she was in the mood for leading a cheer. "Let's get going. We play Deep River next week, so I think we should work on 'They Can Run but They Can't Hide,' " she said, mentioning one of the squad's most rigorous routines.

A chorus of muffled sighs greeted this suggestion. "Mind if we take a vote on that?" Pres asked with a yawn.

Mary Ellen put her hands on her hips and gave him a dirty look. She didn't want to be here any more than anybody else, but she was squad captain, after all. The least Pres could do was back her up. She was on the verge of telling him off when another idea occurred to her. "Olivia," she said sweetly, "could I talk to you for just a second?"

Pres watched the frown in Mary Ellen's wide blue eyes change to a sparkle as she conferred with Olivia, and he began to regret what he'd said. When Mary Ellen got that look, there was no telling what she might have in store for him. Probably some new routine that would require him to lift all four girls at the same time.

Mary Ellen and Olivia spoke quietly for a minute. Olivia laughed and nodded, and then strode over to the bleachers and sat down, her elbows on her knees, her chin in her hands, her brown eyes sparkling as brightly as Mary Ellen's.

Mary Ellen turned to the others. "Okay," she said again. "Besides needing a lot of work, we also need Ardith to whip us into shape. But Ardith isn't here, so — " she stepped back and stretched her arm as master of ceremonies — "presenting, the next best thing!"

Everyone looked at Olivia, who straightened and put her palms flat on her thighs. The sparkle went out of her eyes and was replaced by a look of utter concentration. She cleared her throat and turned those eyes on Nancy.

"I was watching your backbends, Nancy," she

said in the best Ardith Engborg voice she'd ever managed. "They were sloppy, but I'm sure you know that."

Nancy nodded, not sure whether to laugh or feel insulted.

" 'They Can Run' requires you to do several back walkovers, if I'm not mistaken," Olivia went on. "And *I* require them to be perfect, not sloppy."

Walt made a noise that was something between a snort and a chortle, and Olivia immediately shifted her gaze to him. "Walt," she commented quietly, "don't push me. Push yourself, and the squad will be a lot better off."

Walt's chuckling subsided, and he grinned. Slightly embarrassed, he glanced at Angie, who was grinning, too. "I think Olivia missed her calling," Angie whispered. "She could be the star of the drama club."

"It'd sure make her mother a lot happier," Walt whispered back.

Olivia had no intention of joining the legions of unemployed actors, but she was having a great time with this role. She'd taken everyone by surprise, the way she often did with her daring gymnastic moves during a cheer, and it gave her a sense of power. Olivia liked being in control, no matter what the situation.

The others were enjoying her performance as much as she was. Ardith Engborg and Olivia Evans were both small, but the physical resemblance ended there. And Olivia's vocal imitation wasn't really all that great. But there was something in her physical attitude — the way she wrinkled her forehead and cupped her chin in her hands — that reminded the other cheerleaders of their coach.

Singling out Mary Ellen, Olivia said, "I can't be here all the time, you know. You're the captain. It's up to you to keep everybody in line. You've done it before, so do it again." She gave a mischievous smile, totally out of character, and added, "And don't forget, this is a team. Olivia sometimes tries to hog all the spectacular moves, so watch her."

Olivia's put-down of herself made everybody hoot with laughter, and they forgot, for the moment, everything else that had been on their minds. Instead, the six cheerleaders remembered why they'd come to the gym on such a beautiful day — to practice so they'd be the best they could at something they all loved to do.

When Olivia stood up, Pres started clapping. "Bravo!" he shouted. "Encore! Encore!"

"Oh, Pres Tilford." Olivia resumed her Ardith voice and delivered her "encore." "I almost forgot about you. That was easy, since you're only fifty percent here." Grinning at him wickedly, she went on. "I suggest you wipe a certain young woman right out of your mind for the next couple of hours. I know Blake Norton, and if she found out you dropped the ball on account of her, she'd catch the next plane out of Tarenton."

Amid hoots and laughter and applause, Olivia stepped down from the bleachers and took her place with the rest of the squad as they got ready to do the cheer. Her imitation hadn't been perfect, but she'd captured enough of the essence of their coach to remind them of the real thing. For almost two hours afterwards, they worked as if Ardith Engborg were sitting in the bleachers, urging them toward perfection.

The six didn't achieve perfection, but by the time they called it quits for the day, they knew they'd come closer to their usual standard than they had in weeks.

The cheerleaders were elated as they left the school, and no one felt higher than Pres. A couple of hours of hard labor deserved a reward, he thought, and Blake Norton was the best reward he could imagine.

Blake pulled the Porsche into the parking lot just as Pres stepped outside. The minute he saw her, his lips curved into a smile of absolute delight. He shot one hand in the air and trotted toward Blake as if he'd been away from her for two days instead of two hours.

Blake saw the eager smile and felt her stomach sink. She'd been driving around Tarenton almost the entire time Pres had been at practice, working out in her mind exactly what she wanted to say and exactly how to say it. It wasn't going to be easy, but the look on Pres's face and the light in his eyes would make it that much harder.

She reached up, tugged her red knit hat down as if it were armor and she were going into battle, and tapped her fingers on the steering wheel. It was worse than waiting for a late train on a crowded subway platform.

"Hi!" Pres slid into the passenger seat and reached for her. She always smelled so good, especially behind the ears. Nuzzling her there, he whispered, "Did you know that your hat matches this car?"

"You mean I'm color-coordinated?" Blake asked, pretending to be horrified. "That's really out."

"Not to me, it isn't," Pres murmured. "Your hat matches your lips, too." He bent his head and kissed her again.

"Hey," Blake said lightly, "I bet you're starved, huh? Point me to a diner or something and let's get some food."

Pres gave her directions to Gino's Pizza, and then sat back as she put the car into gear and smoothly drove them away. He was feeling great. There was nothing like going from a tough physical workout into the arms of a fantastic girl like Blake. A satisfied smile played over his lips as they rolled along. He liked having Blake drive — he could watch her expressive face. Watching her face had become one of his favorite pastimes.

The only thing bothering Pres at the moment was trying to figure out a way to see Blake more often. They had almost a week left, but then what? She'd be heading back to New York, back to her school, her world. It would be another six weeks until their next break, and Pres didn't know if he could last that long. There was the telephone, of course, but long-distance calls just wouldn't do the trick for six weeks. Talking was a poor substitute for seeing. And touching.

Then, after the two of them had gotten settled at Gino's, Pres had a brainstorm. Snapping his fingers, he said, "Tarenton Fabricators," as if the two words were magic.

"Yeah?" Blake sloshed the ice in her paper cup. "That's where your father works, isn't it?"

"Uh, right, that's where he works," Pres agreed with an ironic smile. He was almost sorry his father hadn't heard it put that way. "Actually, he owns the business."

"I should have guessed," Blake said. "I mean, you don't make millions by punching a time clock, right?"

"Right, but that's not the point." Pres scooted to the edge of the booth and leaned across the table. "You know where Dad is right now?"

"You said he was out of town on business."

"Right! In New York City!"

"No kidding?" Blake thought Pres seemed awfully excited about the whereabouts of his father, considering he wasn't crazy about the man. "Small world, huh?"

"Smaller than I thought," Pres said. "Listen, I told you that Dad's always been disappointed because I wasn't jumping up and down to follow in his footsteps. But now I'm beginning to think the idea has definite possibilities."

"What?" Blake asked skeptically. "You want to become a company man?"

"No, but I could handle it." Pres slid forward even more and squeezed Blake's hand eagerly. "See, Dad goes to New York on business once, sometimes twice a month. And if I'm working for the company, I could probably talk him into letting me go with him. Sort of a way to learn the ropes, you know?"

"I know I'm not stupid," Blake said, "but I just don't get this sudden desire to join Tarenton Fabrics."

"Fabricators," Pres laughed. "And joining it isn't my 'desire,' but getting to New York is. Because you'll be there!" he reminded her. "That way, we'll be able to see each other a couple of times a month until school's out. Then we'll figure out some way to be together during the summer, and after that there's college and we can go to the same one," he finished triumphantly.

"Whoa, hold it," Blake told him. She stared out the window for a second, trying to get her thoughts together. Things were more out of hand than she'd thought. Pres was actually mapping out their future and she had to stop him before he started talking about marriage and babies.

Pushing her pizza aside, Blake took a deep breath. "Pres, I have to talk to you."

CHAPTER

Pres grinned. "I can think of other things I'd rather do with you, but go ahead. Talk."

"Look, I've been thinking about this all afternoon," Blake told him. "Actually, I've been thinking about it almost since I got here."

"Okay, I'll bite," Pres joked. "Thinking about what?"

"About us."

"Hey, me, too!"

"This is serious, Pres," Blake said. Then she rolled her eyes. "I sound like a character from a soap. Oh, well," she said with a shrug, "here goes. Look, I know it was my idea to come to Tarenton. I mean, I really wanted to see you."

"I really wanted to see you, too," Pres told her.

"Yeah, but I don't think you do. See me, that is. You see somebody, but it's not me."

Pres was baffled. There she was, sitting across from him, dark hair, delicious red mouth, great body. What did she mean, he didn't see her? He could hardly take his eyes off her.

But as he started to make a joke out of it, Pres finally noticed the look on Blake's face, and the joke died before it reached his lips. "All right," he said quietly. "Tell me."

Blake hesitated for just a second, took a deep breath, and then plunged into her speech. No sense beating around the bush, she told herself. "Ever since I got here, I feel like . . . like I'm un-real," she explained. "Like I'm a dream — your dream. I think you've got this urge to be in love. So when I dropped in from the sky, it was just perfect timing." She paused and gave him a small smile. "But I'm not so sure you want to be in love with *me*."

"I think I'm a pretty good judge of who I want to be in love with," Pres protested.

"Yeah? So how come you're already mapping out our future?" Blake asked. "You should hear yourself. You're all set to sell out and work for your father just so you can come to New York, and you've got us going to the same college. . . ."

"What's wrong with that?" Pres wanted to know.

"What's wrong with it is you haven't bothered to ask me how *I* feel."

"Well, you did say it was your idea to come here," Pres reminded her, "so I thought your feelings were pretty obvious."

"That's the problem!" Blake said heatedly. "They're *not* obvious, not even to me!"

"Then maybe you shouldn't have come," Pres said.

"Yeah." Blake swallowed hard. "Maybe I shouldn't have."

"Then why did you?"

"Because I wanted to see you," Blake said. "I'm still . . . attracted to you, Pres, but hey! I'm only seventeen. I've got plans, you know?" She ran her fingers through her hair in a gesture of exasperation. "Like, last night, at the party? I felt like I was your wife, or something."

"Is that such a terrible way to feel?"

"Right now it is, yeah," Blake claimed. "And who knows about ten, fifteen years from now? I don't, and I don't think you do, either. But that's how you're acting."

"Yeah, well, sorry," Pres said with a slight edge of sarcasm. "Excuse me for acting the way I feel." He was starting to get angry. Blake was talking to him like he was a twelve-year-old in the throes of his first crush, and it was humiliating. But what made him angrier was that she still hadn't told him how she felt about him. What was this trip to Tarenton all about, anyway?

"Tell me," he said, "why *did* you come here? Were you bored? Did somebody stand you up? Did getting on a plane to Tarenton seem like a real kick? You fly in, fool around with me for a while, and then fly back? Sort of a long one-night stand?"

"Oh, Pres, come off it," Blake told him. "I'm not 'playing' with you, and you know it. What I'm trying to say is I think you want somebody to be in love with, and I just happened to be in the right place at the right time."

"I say you're wrong."

73

"Tough." Blake was angry now, too. "I think you'll change your mind, and that's why I'm leaving. To give you a chance to cool off."

"You're leaving?" Pres asked, completely taken by surprise.

"Right. I'm going to Chicago. There's a flight out tomorrow afternoon," Blake said. "I'll spend some time there and then come back here for a day or two before I go home."

All the anger went out of Pres. He didn't want to lose Blake. He was sure how he felt about her, even if she had doubts. But he knew if he tried to talk her out of going, she'd probably leave even sooner — by bus if she had to. Besides, he didn't want to beg.

"Okay," he said, reaching for her hand again. "If you really want to go, then go."

Blake gave another sigh, of relief this time. "Promise you'll think about what I said?" she asked.

"Sure I will. I'll promise something else, too." Pres smiled his most self-confident of smiles. "I'll still feel the same way when you get back."

Pres left Blake alone in Gino's not because he was angry — although he wasn't too thrilled with her decision to leave — but because he had to meet Patrick and finish up that moving job.

Blake wasn't in the mood to go back to his house and make small talk with Mrs. Tilford. "I'll catch a cab," she told him.

"This isn't New York," Pres reminded her. "You won't find cabs cruising the streets."

"So, I'll call one. Or I'll take a bus." She

grinned. "Tarenton does have buses, doesn't it?"

Pres decided not to argue. If Blake wanted to be alone, then he'd let her be. He didn't like it, but he didn't want to crowd her. Not now.

After Pres left, Blake ordered another soda and sipped it slowly, thinking about the conversation they'd just had. She was sure she'd done the right thing by deciding to go away for a few days, but she was beginning to wonder if she'd made a royal mess by coming to Tarenton in the first place. Maybe it would have been better to stay away. As much as she'd wanted to see Pres, as crazy as she still was about him, she just wasn't ready to make a Big Commitment to any guy. She just hoped Pres, once he cooled down, would realize that he wasn't ready, either.

The cheese on their uneaten pizza had congealed into an unappetizing yellowish glob. Blake was deciding whether or not to have the pizza reheated, when Mary Ellen and Nancy came in.

"Hey, you guys," Blake called. "Come on and help me eat this."

"What are you doing here?" Nancy asked as she and Mary Ellen slid into the booth. "Where's Pres?"

"I'm surprised he left you alone for five minutes," Mary Ellen joked.

"Yeah, well, he had this moving job to do," Blake said. "And you know me, I can't let good food go to waste." She picked up a slice of cold pizza and bit into it.

Nancy and Mary Ellen exchanged glances. Blake liked to think of herself as tough, but she

75

bruised as easily as anyone. And right now, she looked bruised.

"Blake, is something wrong?" Nancy asked. "Did you and Pres have a fight?"

"No, just a disagreement," Blake said with a shrug. She didn't want to go into details, but she didn't want to brush off their concern, either. "Pres and I just need a little time apart, that's all. So I'm going to Chicago tomorrow. I'll see my folks, maybe do some sightseeing. Then I'll come back here."

Nancy was dying to ask what the problem was, but she thought she'd pried enough. "Well," she said, "I'm glad you're coming back to Tarenton, at least. How long will you be in Chicago?"

Before Blake could answer, Vanessa Barlow's voice broke in. "Oh, are you leaving us so soon?" she asked much too sweetly. "That's a shame. But I really can't blame you. I guess Tarenton's too quiet for somebody who's used to all that disgusting big-city noise."

"I happen to like those big-city noises," Blake said. "But there's one thing New York doesn't have, and that's this fantastic cheerleading squad from Tarenton High." She gave Vanessa a sugary smile. "That's why I'm stopping here on my way back from Chicago. To see the squad cheer."

Vanessa shifted her weight from one suede boot to the other and tried to think of something insulting to say. Then she noticed Mary Ellen. "Oh, Chicago!" she exclaimed. "It's supposed to be such an exciting city. I've always wanted to go there. Haven't you, Mary Ellen?" She put a hand over her mouth, pretending to be ashamed of herself. "Oops! I guess I shouldn't have said anything about Chicago."

"Why not?" Mary Ellen asked, trying to keep cool about it.

"Well, Mrs. Gunderson just happened to mention that you had to turn down an opportunity to go there," Vanessa gloated, "and I know how much it must have hurt. I shouldn't have reminded you of it."

"You're so thoughtful, Vanessa," Nancy remarked.

Blake glanced at Mary Ellen, who was trying not to look miserable, and suddenly, Blake had an idea. "Hey, Vanessa, I'm glad you came along," she said. "I'd almost forgotten about Mary Ellen's modeling interview, and you reminded me."

"Isn't it too bad?" Vanessa purred. "Having to turn down something like that must be just awful."

"Yeah, but I was going to say that she doesn't have to turn it down after all," Blake announced.

"I don't?" Mary Ellen asked, startled.

"Not if you don't want to," Blake said. "I mean, all you need is a place to stay, right? And I've got one — my parents' hotel suite!" She turned to Vanessa and grinned. "Isn't it amazing how things work out sometimes? I mean, if you hadn't come along and reminded me of that modeling job, I probably would have gone on to Chicago without even thinking of Mary Ellen. Thanks, Vanessa."

"How does it feel to do a good deed, Vanessa?" Nancy asked dryly.

It obviously didn't feel too great, because Vanessa didn't bother to answer. She merely raised her dark eyebrows at Blake and strode off without a backward glance.

The other three broke into laughter. "Thanks, Blake," Mary Ellen said gratefully. "The look on her face makes turning down that interview a little easier."

"But you don't have to turn it down," Blake said. "I'm serious. You can come to Chicago with me."

Mary Ellen stared at her.

"Really," Blake went on. "My parents always rent a suite, so there'll be plenty of room. And food's no problem — they're always willing to treat my friends. What do you say?"

Mary Ellen went on staring until Nancy nudged her. "If you're worried about all those workouts we scheduled," Nancy said, "forget it. Nobody would expect you to stay for them, not even me." She turned to Blake. "I think she's in shock," she explained. "But don't worry, she says yes. Right, Mary Ellen?"

Mary Ellen finally came out of her trance. She stood up, reached across the table, and gave Blake an awkward hug. "Right!" she cried, her face breaking into an ear-to-ear smile. "I say *yes*!"

On Monday morning, Mary Ellen's room looked as if a cyclone had hit it. Clothes were strewn and draped on every available surface; shoes were scattered around the floor; and the top of the bureau was covered with scarves, makeup, and jewelry.

Mary Ellen, still in her bathrobe, stared at the single, small suitcase she was packing, and wondered how she could possibly fit everything into it.

"You'll only be there two days," Gemma reminded her from her perch on the bed. "All you need is something to sleep in, something to wear to the interview, and something to wear around town. That's three things."

"I know!" Mary Ellen cried. "But which three? Anyway, I should probably take more, just in case."

"Just in case what?" Gemma asked.

"Oh, you know. What if I spill something on my interview outfit? I'll need another one." Actually, Mary Ellen had a secret fantasy that Mr. Seltzman would sign her on the spot and then ask her to dinner to meet some important clients. But she was keeping that fantasy to herself.

Still, it wasn't a totally impossible dream. She'd called the Futura Modeling Agency an hour ago, and Mr. Seltzman had sounded very friendly and pleased that she was coming. Her appointment was for eleven-thirty Wednesday morning, and he'd told her to keep lunch open. Lunch? She'd keep the entire day open if it meant getting hired.

"It's too bad Mr. Whatsit can't see you now," Gemma said. "You look beautiful."

"What? I don't even have any makeup on," Mary Ellen laughed. But a quick glance in the mirror told her she didn't need any makeup. Her cheeks were flushed a very becoming shade of pink, and her eyes were bright with excitement. Bless Blake, she thought. She grinned at her reflection and turned back to the jumbled room, determined to decide, finally, what to take and what to leave behind. Fortunately, the phone rang, and she put the decision off for a few more minutes.

"It's Patrick," Gemma announced. "Have you told him you're going?"

"No," Mary Ellen said as she went into the hall. "I guess I'd better do it now."

As it turned out, Patrick already knew. He'd heard the news from Pres. What's more, since he and Pres had another job scheduled for that afternoon, they were driving Blake and Mary Ellen to the airport in the van. "So this isn't a good-bye call," he said lightly. "It's a congratulations call."

"Really?" Mary Ellen hadn't been sure how he'd react. "Do you mean it, Patrick?"

"Come on," he said softly. "Didn't I tell you I wish you the best?"

Mary Ellen smiled into the phone. "Yes, you did. Thank you, Patrick. It means a lot, knowing you're on my side."

"I'll always be on your side, Mary Ellen," he told her. "And don't forget. I'll be here when you come back."

"I know," she said. What she didn't say was that once she got her big break, she'd probably never come back.

But Mary Ellen didn't have to say it — Patrick already knew.

Later, at the airport, it was all Patrick could

do to keep smiling and making conversation. Watching Mary Ellen, her face still flushed with anticipation, he felt helpless. She was slipping away from him — if not this time, then surely another time soon — and he couldn't think of any way to hold her back. All he could do was let her go and hope that she'd have enough sense to come back on her own.

Pres kept himself slightly aloof from all the small talk. He was still miffed that Blake didn't trust his feelings for her, but if she wanted to put them through some stupid test, he'd go along with it. Nothing was going to change in two days, and when she got back to Tarenton, she'd have to realize he was sincere.

Nancy was in Hillsborough, working with Eric, but Angie, Chris, Walt, and Olivia had come to the airport to see the two girls off. When the flight was called, Angie reached out and hugged Mary Ellen. "Good luck, Melon," she whispered excitedly.

"Right. Knock 'em dead," Walt said. He gave her a hug and so did Olivia. Chris cleared his throat and recited a "Christopher Page Original": "Farewell, Mary Ellen and Blake/ Off to that windy city by the lake/ And when your wandering days are done/ Remember in your hearts that Tarenton's Number One."

"Tarenton?" Blake asked, laughing. "What about New York?"

Chris grinned. "Couldn't find a good rhyme for it."

"Thanks, you guys," Mary Ellen told them. She picked up her carry-on bag and slung her purse over her shoulder. "Chicago, here we come!"

"Not if we don't hurry," Blake said. "They just gave the final call." She turned to Pres and gave him a jaunty smile. "See you in a few days, okay?"

"I'll be waiting," Pres said. He bent down and brushed her mouth with his lips. "You can count on that."

Just before Mary Ellen disappeared through the boarding gate, she turned back and glanced at Patrick. He was watching her, his hands stuffed in his pockets. But when he saw her turn, he freed one hand and raised it in the air, giving her a thumbs-up signal. Mary Ellen responded with a bright smile and a quick wave.

Pres noticed. "She's looking good," he said.

Patrick nodded. "So's Blake."

Pres hunched his shoulders and stared at his feet. "If they're looking so good, how come we're feeling so bad?" he asked.

"Sounds like a country-western song," Patrick remarked. Then he clapped Pres on the shoulder and grinned. "Come on, we've got a job. Let's go lift some furniture and sweat the misery right out of us."

Together, they left the airport terminal, reaching the van at the same moment the silver plane lifted into the sky, heading for Chicago.

CHAPTER

8

On Wednesday morning, while Nancy was showering herself awake, she thought of Mary Ellen. This was the day. In a few short hours, Mary Ellen would be entering the office of a big-time Chicago modeling agency, ready to pit her face and body against hundreds of other faces and bodies.

Nancy had never totally sympathized with Mary Ellen's urge to be a model. In the Goldstein family, modeling was viewed as a mindless, fluff occupation, and some of that view had rubbed off on Nancy. In fact, Nancy and Mary Ellen rarely saw eye-to-eye on anything. Still, since Nancy knew how much this chance meant to Mary Ellen, she found herself shivering with anticipation in spite of the warm, misty spray of the shower.

At the same time that morning, Olivia, having turned down her mother's suggestion of hot oatmeal for breakfast, peeled a banana, and wondered if Mary Ellen had mentally prepared herself for this interview. That was the most important thing, in Olivia's opinion. She didn't want to be a model any more than Nancy. But she knew all about wanting to be the best at something, and nine times out of ten, she knew it was your mind that could mess you up. You had to shut out everything and everybody. You had to focus only on what was in front of you, whether it was a midair flip or a person who could decide your future.

Mary Ellen could do it, Olivia thought, as long as she concentrated. She almost envied her — at least she had something to concentrate *on*. The only thing in front of Olivia that morning was an empty day and an argument with Walt about how to spend it.

Angie wasn't bothered by thoughts of mental preparedness, and she didn't question whether modeling was a worthwhile career. She simply wished Mary Ellen the best. The thought that all she could do was cross her fingers made her feel rather helpless.

She greeted her mother's hairdressing customers; made a date to meet Chris later in the day; straightened up her room; bantered with her brothers; and kept her eye on the clock, her watch, or whatever timepiece was closest. Angie was a hummer, but this morning, instead of humming, she kept murmuring an improvised cheer which consisted mainly of the words, *Go, Mary Ellen, go!*

In Room 1717 of the Drake Hotel in Chicago,

Mary Ellen Kirkwood stared at her reflection in the mirror and watched her face break into a smile. Maybe she was happy because she had been invited to this interview and hadn't had to beg for it. Or maybe the combined good wishes of her fellow cheerleaders had somehow traveled from Tarenton to Chicago along with her. Whatever the reason for her glee, Mary Ellen had never felt so sure of herself, so positive that things were going to go her way.

"I've got to stop grinning," she said to Blake, who was eating croissants from the breakfast tray delivered by room service. "I don't want to look cocky."

Blake spread plum preserves on one of the flaky rolls. "When you've got it, flaunt it," she said with a chuckle. "Actually, you don't look cocky. You look happy, like somebody just gave you a Christmas present in July."

"That's it," Mary Ellen said. "That's exactly how I feel." She spread her arms to indicate the beautiful room with its velvety thick carpet, handsome teak furniture, and panoramic view of Lake Michigan. "This is part of the present. If it hadn't been for you, I probably couldn't have come. Or else I'd have had to stay in some cubicle at the 'Y.'" She spun around, laughing. "But this place has so much class! It makes me feel classy!"

"You are classy. You don't need a hotel room to prove it," Blake told her. "But I guess I see what you mean. Anyway, don't thank me, thank my parents. I gotta give Rose and William credit — they do things in style."

Mary Ellen glanced curiously at Blake, who

always sounded slightly sarcastic when she mentioned her parents. The Nortons — he, tall and imposing; she, short and imposing — had been surprised but pleasant when their daughter had arrived ahead of schedule, with a friend in tow, and taken over the sitting room of their hotel suite.

"I like your parents," Mary Ellen said now. "They could have freaked out when we showed up, but they were really cool about it."

Blake grinned wryly. "Cool's the word, all right. They don't exactly radiate warmth, as you may have noticed."

"But they've got all these conferences and seminars," Mary Ellen pointed out. "They're busy."

"You don't have to tell me that," Blake said, curling up on the soft beige couch. "They're always busy. Of course, even if they had a lot of free time, they wouldn't spend it with me. I don't think they need me."

"Sure they do," Mary Ellen argued. "They just don't show it." She started to say more, but changed her mind. She didn't know Blake or her parents well enough to second-guess any of them. Besides, she thought it would be exciting to have a mother and father with careers, not just jobs.

Mary Ellen realized, however, that Blake, who was sipping orange juice and trying to appear nonchalant, would probably welcome two doting parents. Mary Ellen decided to try a joke. "Well," she said, "if you need to be needed, there's always Pres."

"Very funny," Blake said. "Pres doesn't need me. Pres just *needs*, period."

Mary Ellen knew something about Pres's needs, too, and she started to laugh.

Blake lifted her juice glass in a toast. "To Preston Tilford III!" she said. "A truly needy case!" She finished the juice and shook her head. "I shouldn't put Pres down. He's one of the greatest guys I've ever met. The timing's just not right, you know?"

"I know," Mary Ellen said. "Anyway, if Pres doesn't need you, I do. I need you, Blake Norton, to get off that couch, get dressed — not in anything too eye-catching — and come with me to the Futura Modeling Agency."

Blake stayed where she was. "What for?" she asked. "You don't need anybody to hold your hand. You're not scared."

"Maybe not," Mary Ellen said with a grin. "But when Mr. Martin Seltzman hands me a contract and says, 'You're hired,' I'll need somebody to celebrate with, right?"

"Right!"

In high spirits, the two girls spent the next hour deciding which outfit Mary Ellen should wear when she set out to conquer Chicago.

During that same hour, the only thing Pres felt like conquering was the urge to chuck the whole moving business and spend the days until Blake came back holed up in his room with his headset jammed on to block out the rest of the world.

Unfortunately, he had a partner to consider. Patrick, Pres knew, would not have looked too kindly on any suggestion that they turn down work. In fact, he probably would have dissolved the partnership then and there.

"What's the job?" Pres asked as he and Patrick drove across town in the van.

"Somebody named Priscilla Crandall," Patrick said. "She's been staying at a motel and storing her stuff, but she finally found an apartment near the Little Folks Nursery School. That's where she works."

Terrific, Pres thought. A nursery school teacher. Probably fifty years old. Probably'll talk their ears off. Probably'll offer them milk and cookies instead of soda and sandwiches. He groaned softly at the image.

"Hey, come on, man," Patrick said. "Watching you mope about Blake is about as exciting as watching hair grow. Why don't you loosen up?"

"I've tried," Pres protested. "And I've failed. It seems like all I can do is sit and wait for her to come back."

"It's only a couple of days," Patrick reminded him.

"I know. It's just that I don't know what'll happen when she does get back. That's what has me so uptight." Pres sighed and stared out at the gray day. "I mean, do I have to stand on my head to prove to her that I'm crazy about her?"

"I hear you," Patrick said with a rueful smile. "I know exactly where you're coming from."

"Oh, right." Pres felt slightly ashamed of himself. After all, Patrick faced a similar problem — almost all the time — with Mary Ellen. "How do you handle it?" he asked. "What's your secret for getting through the day?"

"There is no secret," Patrick confessed as he turned the van into the warehouse parking lot. "I guess whatever takes your mind off your girl friend is the secret. For me, right now, it's Priscilla Crandall's furniture." He brought the van to a stop and pointed. "There she is now. Come on, let's go meet the lady and hope she doesn't have a grand piano in that warehouse."

Still slouching in his seat, Pres stared idly through the windshield. Then he straightened up and looked again.

The only person outside the storage warehouse was a slender, leggy young woman whose hair swirled around her head like a reddish-blonde halo. She wore close-fitting jeans tucked into high suede boots, and a down vest over a bright orange turtleneck. Pres would have bet even money that her eyes were green.

Priscilla Crandall, nursery school teacher, was nothing like Pres had expected.

The look on Pres's face wasn't lost on Patrick. "I see you've found *your* secret for getting through the day," he commented dryly. "You recover fast, don't you."

The receptionist at the Futura Modeling Agency took Mary Ellen's name and smiled warmly. "Mr. Seltzman's expecting you," she purred. "He's on an important call right now, but as soon as he's free, I'll let him know you're here."

"Thank you," Mary Ellen said.

"May I get you some coffee or tea?" the receptionist inquired.

"Not for me, thanks." Mary Ellen turned to Blake. "But maybe my friend. . . ?"

"Sure," Blake piped up. "Tea with lemon would be great."

"Fine." The receptionist smiled again and walked down the hall, leaving a scent of musk in her wake.

Mary Ellen took a deep breath and sat down beside Blake. "How do I look?" she asked.

Blake studied her. After a lot of discussion, they'd decided that Mary Ellen shouldn't appear *too* casual, even though most models walked around in jeans or sweat suits. So Mary Ellen had compromised, choosing a pair of well-cut gray corduroy pants; a silky violet blouse; and a loosely woven, sleeveless gray sweater vest. "You look great. Oh, thanks," she said as she was handed a cup of steaming tea. She waited until the receptionist was seated behind her desk again. "This place is not what I expected," she muttered under her breath.

"What's wrong with it?" Mary Ellen eyed the high-tech furnishings of the nearly empty waiting area. "It looks fabulous to me. You should have seen that place I went to in New York. It was like Grand Central Station — phones ringing, people coming and going, everybody watching the clock."

Exactly, Blake thought. It was busy. This place was extremely quiet and extremely plush. They must be doing something right to pay for offices like this, but still, it just didn't feel like it should have.

"Look," she said, "if this guy Seltzer — "

"Seltzman," Mary Ellen hissed.

"Right. If he whips out a contract or something and asks you to sign on the dotted line, don't do it. Not right away," Blake advised. "Tell him you have to check with your agent first."

"I don't have an agent," Mary Ellen reminded her. "He knows that."

"Okay." Blake was undaunted. "Tell him you want your lawyer to look everything over."

"I don't have a lawyer, either."

"I know that, and you know that," Blake said. "But Mr. Seltzer doesn't know that. Anyway, it'll make you seem more professional. Everybody has an agent or a lawyer these days. He'll expect that."

"You're right," Mary Ellen agreed. "I didn't even think of that. The last thing I want to do is seem like a hick."

"Right. You want to seem like a winner."

Just then, a muted buzz sounded on the desk. The receptionist picked up the phone, murmured something into it, and then smiled at Mary Ellen. "Miss Kirkwood? Mr. Seltzman will see you now."

Mary Ellen stood up and took another deep breath. This was it. This was the chance she'd been waiting for, and she was ready to take that chance and make the most of it.

She picked up her portfolio case and turned to Blake. "Wish me luck," she said.

Blake grinned and gave the "V for Victory" sign. "Knock 'em dead, Mary Ellen."

The receptionist, smile in place, was waiting at an open door. Shoulders straight, head high, Mary Ellen followed her inside, looking more like a winner than she ever had in her life.

CHAPTER

Martin Seltzman, who looked to be some-where in his thirties, rose from behind an enor-mous mahogany desk and extended a hand as Mary Ellen entered his office. He had small brown eyes that took in her face and figure in one cool, appraising glance.

"Miss Kirkwood, glad you're here," he said. "Sit down, please."

"Thank you." Mary Ellen shook his hand and took the chair he indicated. "I'm glad to be here."

"I'll bet." A smile flickered across his lips. "This kind of thing doesn't happen to high school kids too often, as you probably know."

"No, I'm sure it doesn't," Mary Ellen agreed. But it's happening to me, she thought, and sat up a little straighter.

"Okay, so, let's get right down to business," Mr. Seltzman said. "Futura's a young company — just three years old. But we're on the rise, and we're taking a good number of ambitious young women like you right up with us. Have you caught the new Second Skin commercial?"

Mary Ellen vaguely recalled an ad she'd seen on television featuring a sultry model reclining in a tub filled with Second Skin Bath Oil. She nodded.

"That's Monica James," Seltzman told her. "She got her start at Futura. And here." He pushed a magazine across the desk, turning it so Mary Ellen could see another sultry woman draped across the cover. The name of the magazine was *Fashion Fix*. Mary Ellen had never heard of the magazine, but it looked very slick.

"Adrienne Alexander," Seltzman said. "She was another one of ours." He flipped through a few more magazines, showing Mary Ellen other models. None of them seemed to be with Futura anymore, and Mary Ellen assumed they'd all gone on to bigger and better things, like New York. Like you will, she told herself.

When he finished, Seltzman sat back in his chair. His smile clicked on again, rather like a flashbulb. "So this is what we've done in three years. What do you think?"

"I think it sounds wonderful," Mary Ellen said. "I've wanted to be a model ever since I can remember." Don't gush, she told herself. She reached for her case and slid it across his desk. "I suppose you'd like to know what I've done. Of course, it isn't a very big portfolio." She caught herself apologizing and stopped. "But once I make it in this business — "

"If you make it, you won't need a portfolio,"

Seltzman broke in. He pulled out the meager pile of photographs and flipped through them quickly and silently.

Mary Ellen cleared her throat. "Do you want me to walk?" she asked.

"What?"

"Walk," she repeated. "I went on an interview in New York once and they asked me to walk — to see how I move."

"I know you can move," Seltzman said, dismissing her suggestion with a wave of his hand. "I saw that commercial." He slipped the photos back into the case and gave her another once-over with his small brown eyes. "I don't think there's any question that you have a future in this business," he told her. "We can get you work, if you want it. Do you want it?"

Mary Ellen was stunned. Was he really saying what she thought he was saying? Was he really ready to hire her?

"Yes, I want it," she said calmly, as if her heart weren't thudding like a drum. "That's why I'm here."

Suddenly, though, Mary Ellen couldn't hold back any longer. She had to know, to be sure this wasn't a dream. "Mr. Seltzman? Are you offering me a job?"

"A job?" The quick smile came and went. "I'm ready to offer you a three-year exclusive contract."

Mary Ellen could think of nothing to say but, "Oh." If she'd been standing, she would have had to sit down.

"Of course, you won't find yourself on a magazine cover next week," Seltzman pointed out. "Nobody starts at the top, not even Monica James."

Mary Ellen didn't consider lying in a bathtub full of Second Skin being at the top, but it was a lot farther up the ladder than she was now. "I've always wanted — will I be able to do runway modeling?"

"No question. Maybe not at first, but eventually." Seltzman cleared his throat. "In the meantime, we get you lots of what I call our 'bread-and-butter' work. It's not glamorous, but it puts food on the table — your table and ours."

As he went on talking about bread-and-butter work Martin Seltzman slid several catalogs across the desk for Mary Ellen to look at. But Mary Ellen didn't really see the catalogs, and she barely heard Seltzman's voice. Her mind was still reeling with the fantastic knowledge that she'd actually been offered a modeling job. Not just one job, either, but three years' worth of jobs.

Three years! Just imagine where she'd be in three years. Pictures kept flashing through Mary Ellen's mind: There she was, striding down a runway in a stunning outfit by one of America's top designers, while flashbulbs popped and applause burst around her. There she was again, in a famous photographer's studio, posing for the cover of *Vogue*. Next, she saw herself in Paris or the Bahamas, taping a commercial that would make her famous across the country.

It's not a dream anymore, she told herself. It's a dream come true.

Mary Ellen was so carried away by visions of

her future that a full minute passed before she realized Martin Seltzman had stopped talking. She glanced up, saw him watching her, and felt her cheeks get hot. Really professional, Mary Ellen, she told herself. Daydreaming in the middle of the most important interview of your life.

"I'm sorry," she told him, still blushing. "I'm afraid I wasn't listening."

Seltzman gave a short laugh and a quick glance at his watch. "No problem," he said. "You're overwhelmed — that's understandable." He pointed to a thick sheaf of papers on his desk. "I was talking about your contract. I'd really hoped we could go over it at lunch, but something has come up and there's just not going to be time."

Mary Ellen took the contract, holding it in her hands as if it were an exquisite piece of china she mustn't drop. "That's all right," she said. "I know you're busy."

"Right. So what I thought was, you take it, look it over, and get back to me, say, this afternoon." Seltzman checked his watch again. "No. To tell you the truth, tomorrow would be better. You have any questions, you call me tomorrow. How does that sound?"

"It sounds fine," Mary Ellen said. Actually, she was ready to sign the contract right then and there, but Mr. Seltzman seemed in such a hurry she didn't want to risk annoying him. Besides, Blake was probably right. Signing a contract without even reading it wouldn't look professional at all. "I'll have my lawyer look it over and get back to you tomorrow," she told him.

"Well, it's a standard contract," Seltzman said

as he stood up. "Your lawyer won't find any surprises in it. Just tell him not to take too long, Mary Ellen. We've got calls coming in every day, people screaming for models. I'd hate to see you miss out because your lawyer dragged his feet."

"Oh, don't worry, that won't happen," Mary Ellen assured him. "I'll call you tomorrow." She stood up, too, clutching the contract and the catalogs, and held out her free hand. "Thank you, Mr. Seltzman," she said. "I'm very excited. I can't wait to get to work."

"That's what we like to hear," Seltzman said, shaking her hand and then ushering her to the door. "I'll talk to you tomorrow, Mary Ellen."

Outside his door, Mary Ellen stood a moment and looked around. Pretty soon, she told herself, this place will seem like home. You'll walk in past the receptionist, head straight into Martin Seltzman's office, and say, "Okay, Marty, what's on for today?" And he'll say something like, "Mary Ellen, am I glad to see you! A cover shot just came up, and yours is the face they want. You're hot, Mary Ellen. Didn't I tell you it would happen?"

"Miss Kirkwood?" The soft-voiced receptionist was standing in front of Mary Ellen, a curious look on her face. "Is there something I can do for you?"

Mary Ellen gave herself a little shake and pushed the fantasy from her mind. "No," she said with a brilliant smile. "I'm fine. Everything's absolutely fine!"

Still smiling, Mary Ellen walked down the hall and into the waiting room. Blake was in the same chair, leafing impatiently through a magazine. When she saw Mary Ellen, she tossed the magazine onto a smoked-glass table and stood up. "Well?"

Mary Ellen held out the contract. "Look at this!" she said, trying not to squeal with excitement.

Blake looked. "What is it?"

"A contract!" Mary Ellen took a deep breath and suppressed a giggle. "Blake, he gave me a contract!"

"You're kidding!" Blake stared at the papers. "Talk about fast work. Hey," she said suddenly, "you mean you signed it already?"

"No, he didn't have time to go over it with me," Mary Ellen told her. "But I'm going to. There's no way I'm going to let this slip out of my hands. Oh, Blake, can you believe it? This is the most fantastic thing that's ever happened to me!"

"Yeah, I'll bet!" Blake tried to sound as enthusiastic as Mary Ellen, but inside, she was skeptical. She just didn't believe in overnight success stories. "Well, listen, this is terrific," she said. "Let's uh . . . let's go someplace and read it, try to figure out what it says."

"Who cares what it says?" Mary Ellen laughed. "Let's go out into the Windy City and celebrate!"

While Blake and Mary Ellen were looking for a place to celebrate in Chicago, Olivia and Walt were staring at the vast expanse of ice at the Tarenton Indoor Rink.

It had been Olivia's idea to go skating, and since Walt hadn't been able to suggest anything

99

better to do, he'd agreed. It wasn't that he didn't like to ice-skate. He just wasn't in the mood for it. And since his heart wasn't in it, his legs and feet weren't in it, either. He fell so many times he stopped counting, while Olivia whizzed past him, a graceful bundle of energy in her lavender down vest and bright yellow legwarmers.

Finally, fed up with Olivia's effortless pirouettes and with his own unusual clumsiness, Walt had skated shakily over to one of the benches placed at regular intervals around the rink.

Olivia took one more turn around the rink before joining him. She was disgusted and wanted to make sure she had her temper in check before she said anything. What was the matter with Walt, anyway? Ever since the vacation had started, he'd been acting like the entire world — including her — was one big bore. That just wasn't like Walt.

Suddenly, a thought occurred to her, something she hadn't even considered. She cut across the ice, nearly colliding with Vanessa Barlow, who gave her a dirty look, and glided easily up to Walt.

"Are you sick?" she demanded.

Walt stared at her, then slowly put his hand on his forehead. "I didn't want you to find out this way," he said dramatically. "But don't worry, it's not catching."

"Don't you joke around with me about being sick, Walt Manners!" Olivia's dark eyes were flashing. "I don't laugh at sick jokes!"

Walt stared at his skates. "Sorry," he said

sincerely. "Really. No, I'm not sick. I'm in perfect health. Honest."

Way to go, Walt, he told himself. You have a real knack for putting your foot in it. He reached up and took Olivia's hand. "Olivia? I'm really sorry. Don't be mad, I'm just . . . I don't know."

Olivia sat down beside him and leaned her head on his shoulder. "I'm not mad anymore," she said. "I just want to know what's wrong."

"Ah, it's nothing," Walt said. "I guess I'm not very self-reliant sometimes, that's all."

"Why do you think that?"

"Because I keep wishing something exciting would happen," he said. "And it doesn't work that way. You have to make things happen. You know, I actually miss working out with the squad."

Olivia nodded. "It's funny, isn't it? A few days of freedom and we don't know what to do with ourselves." She took his hand and squeezed it. "Hey, I have an idea. Why don't you throw that party? Remember when Ardith said we'd be free for midyear recess? We all decided you should have a party."

"Yeah, but Pres already had one," Walt reminded her.

"So? Who says we can't have another one?" Olivia said.

"You're right," Walt agreed. "I'll check with Mom and Dad and see which night'll be best. Let's make it a real blast," he said. "Let's invite everybody."

"Fine with me," Olivia said. Then, looking out at the ice, she changed her mind. "Everyone but Vanessa."

Vanessa had just bumped into Angie, who had come skating with Chris. Vanessa made a futile effort to stay upright, clutched at air, and finally landed on her rear.

Angie was not the best skater in the world, so she knew how silly it felt to suddenly find yourself sitting on the ice while everyone else whirled around you. When Angie fell, she laughed, but Vanessa had too high an opinion of herself to find the situation funny. She was humiliated and outraged.

Angie allowed herself three seconds to enjoy the spectacle of Vanessa Barlow sitting in the middle of an ice rink. Then her better instincts took over, and she held out her hand.

"Cold, huh?" She laughed.

Vanessa didn't return the laugh. She waved Angie's hand away and struggled to her feet, muttering something about klutzes, and she obviously didn't mean herself. Then she seemed to take real notice of Angie, and her frown changed to a sneer.

"Oh, it's you," she remarked. "I'm surprised you're here having fun, Angie. I thought you'd be in mourning."

"Why?" Angie asked. "Did some disaster happen?"

"Well, it's not a disaster for everyone, naturally," Vanessa said. "But I certainly didn't expect a member of the Varsity Squad to look so happy, considering. . . ."

"Considering what? Vanessa, what are you talking about?"

"I'm talking about your coach, Mrs. Engborg," Vanessa said with a shake of her head.

Angie's mouth went dry. "Did something happen to Ardith?" she managed to ask.

"Happen? Well, not exactly." Vanessa tossed her hair back and smirked. "I guess she finally got fed up with Tarenton High, not to mention the Tarenton High Varsity Cheerleading Squad, so she decided to look for greener pastures. She's taking another job, at another school," Vanessa announced with great satisfaction.

CHAPTER

At first, Angie felt just relief. She'd been envisioning a car wreck or a plane crash. Once it was clear that nothing like that had happened to Ardith, she laughed. "I don't believe that for a minute, Vanessa."

"Oh, dear." Vanessa put a hand over her mouth and shook her head again. "I guess she didn't want you to know yet. But it's true. I heard her tell my father — and these are her exact words — 'I've been in one place too long. It's time for me to move on.'"

"I still don't believe it," Angie said. Ardith Engborg leaving Tarenton High? Leaving the squad, when it meant so much to her? When she meant so much to it? It couldn't be true. "Vanessa, I know you hate us because you didn't make the squad," Angie told her in a shaky voice. "And I don't really mind if you hate us.

But please, you can't go around making up rumors just to prove it."

"Rumors?" Vanessa looked indignant. "I'm just telling you what I heard. If you think I've made it up, then you're welcome to ask my father. Better yet," she suggested, "ask Ardith."

"I will," Angie said. "You can bet I will!" But she was talking to herself. Having dropped her bomb, Vanessa didn't wait around for the explosion. She was soon halfway across the rink.

Angie stood on the ice, unable to move or to think. It can't be true, she kept telling herself. Meanwhile, another part of her kept asking, But what if it is?

"Angie? Honey?" Chris slipped his arm around her waist. "You okay?"

Angie shook her head mutely, and then grabbed his hand, pulling him across the ice. "I've got to talk to Walt and Olivia. Come on!"

Olivia and Walt had been watching the little scene between Angie and Vanessa, so when Angie skated up to them, Chris in tow, they were prepared for yet another outrageous Vanessa Barlow story. But they were completely unprepared for what Angie told them.

"I don't believe it," Olivia said flatly when Angie finished. "I have to admit, it's more imaginative than Vanessa's usual rumors, but it's still a lie."

"Sure it is," Walt agreed. "Ardith wouldn't leave Tarenton. And even if she did, she wouldn't do it without telling us."

"That's what I think," Angie said, nervously

picking miniscule balls of yarn off her mittens. "But I want to find out for sure."

"But how?" Olivia asked. "Vanessa cleverly forgot to mention that her father's out of town at some education convention, so you can't ask him."

"He'd probably back his little girl, anyway," Walt said. "Or else he'd refuse to discuss it."

"I'm not going to bother with Dr. Barlow," Angie told them. "I'm going straight to the source. I'm going to ask Mrs. Engborg."

But when Angie got home and called Ardith's number later that day, there was no answer. She waited an hour and tried again. Still no answer.

"Maybe she went to the movies or something," Chris suggested. He'd never seen Angie so upset, so close to panic, and he wasn't sure how to handle it. "Hey, why don't we go, too? Maybe we'll see her there. And even if we don't, it'll take your mind off it."

Angie didn't even bother to turn down the suggestion. "I'll call Nancy," she said, dialing the phone. "Maybe she knows something."

Nancy was dressing for a date with Eric, and she was running late, but Angie's news made her forget the time. As she listened, she caught herself trying to imagine what the squad would be like without Ardith. It wasn't a pretty picture. Then she pushed that picture out of her mind. "Be realistic, Angie," she said. "Walt's right. Mrs. Engborg would never do anything like that without telling us."

"I don't think she would, either," Angie said.

"But maybe she just hasn't gotten around to it yet. Nancy, I want to know if it's true or not!"

"So do I," Nancy admitted. "Listen, why don't you call Mrs. Oetjen? The principal of Tarenton High ought to know if one of her teachers is leaving, right?"

"Right!" Angie breathed a sigh of relief, said good-bye to Nancy, and immediately started looking for Mrs. Oetjen's number. She found it, dialed, and listened miserably as Mr. Oetjen told her that his wife was attending the same convention as Dr. Barlow, and wouldn't be back for another three days.

Declining Chris's suggestion that they go to a movie, Angie stationed herself by the kitchen phone, dialing Mrs. Engborg's number every half hour. At ten, she walked Chris to the door, gave him a distracted kiss, and made herself a cup of tea. Deep down, she knew that she shouldn't panic, not when all she had to go on was Vanessa Barlow's word. But just as deep down, she knew she couldn't relax until she uncovered the truth. Except for Chris and her family, the Varsity Squad meant more to Angie than anything, and she couldn't even imagine what her world would be like without it.

Every time Blake looked at Mary Ellen, she thought of that old phrase, *grinning from ear to ear*. Mary Ellen hadn't stopped smiling since the two of them had left the Futura Modeling Agency, and Blake was beginning to wonder if her friend's cheek muscles were ever going to recover.

Speaking of recovering, Blake thought, what about my feet? For some idiotic reason, she'd worn new boots today, and after almost an hour of walking, her left heel and right big toe had developed blisters that felt as big as quarters. Normally, she loved to walk, especially on clear, cold days like this. But her feet really were killing her, and besides, she wanted to get a look at that contract. Not to put Mary Ellen down or anything, but Blake still had trouble believing that someone so inexperienced would be offered a three-year contract without having to prove herself first.

"Hey, Mary Ellen," she called, "let's find someplace to eat. I'm famished."

Mary Ellen stopped inspecting a window display of jewelry and looked at Blake, who was limping along a few yards back. "You look more hurt than hungry," she said with a laugh.

"I'm both," Blake groaned. Peering at the jewelry, which featured a lot of gold and diamonds draped on black and velvet and lit by tiny spotlights, she whistled softly and shook her head. "Come on, Mary Ellen, this stuff is for the ultra-ultra rich."

"I know; I was just imagining," Mary Ellen said.

"Imagining what?"

"Imagining what it'll be like when I go in there someday and don't even have to ask the price of anything." Mary Ellen laughed again. "I know it won't happen tomorrow, but it'll happen, Blake!"

"I believe you," Blake said. "But can't we eat something before you make your first million?"

After walking another half block, they found a trendy-looking eatery that served gelato. The place, a slick tiled and mirrored version of an ice-cream parlor, and the light Italian ice cream, which came in every flavor imaginable, suited Mary Ellen's mood and appetite. She feasted happily on two scoops of chocolate hazelnut gelato while Blake tried to make sense of the Futura contract.

"You really do need a lawyer for this kind of thing," Blake commented. "It sounds like it was written in old English!"

"I don't care what language it's written in, just as long as it's mine," Mary Ellen claimed.

"Yeah, well, if you sign this, you'll be Futura's, body and soul." Blake scanned one of the paragraphs and frowned. "Here. It says something about how Futura has total control over all of your assignments. Which means that for three years, you have to do what they say. Doesn't that bother you a little?"

"Nope," Mary Ellen said blithely. "Why should it?"

"Well. . . ." Blake ran her fingers through her hair. "I mean, suppose you do some work and then somebody calls you for a modeling job. But you can't do it because . . . I don't know . . . Futura already has you booked, or they don't think it would be good for your career, or something like that. You'd have to say no."

"I see what you mean," Mary Ellen said. "But

I really don't see a problem, Blake. Sure, maybe I'd have to turn down a job, but I'd still have one — with Futura."

"What if you liked the one you turned down better?" Blake persisted.

Mary Ellen swallowed some ice cream and shrugged. "I guess I'd tell Futura about it and see if they'd let me do it."

"Yeah? And what if they wouldn't?"

"Blake!" Mary Ellen laughed again, but she was beginning to get annoyed. Why was Blake being so picky? "Why wouldn't they let me do it? Why wouldn't they let me do something that would be good for my career? After all, they'd still be getting their commission, so what difference would it make?"

"No difference, I guess," Blake admitted. "Except according to this contract, *they* decide what's good for your career. And," she went on, slapping the thick set of papers on the table, "what's *really* good for your career might not be good for Futura."

Mary Ellen scooped out her last spoonful of gelato, swallowed it, and then picked up the precious contract. "I just don't understand what you're getting at, Blake. I've just had the most incredible break of my life, and you're trying to ruin it for me."

"Hey, I'm sorry," Blake said, backing off. "Really. Me and my big mouth. I'll keep it shut from now on, how's that?"

Mary Ellen shook her head and smiled. "It's all right. I didn't mean to jump on you like that. I'm just so excited, I can hardly sit still!" She giggled and then leaned across the small table. "The other reason I can't sit still is I have to find a bathroom, quick!"

While Mary Ellen was in the bathroom, Blake finished her ice cream, wishing it were a pastrami sandwich instead. Then she leafed through the catalogs Martin Seltzman had given to Mary Ellen. By the time Mary Ellen got back to the table, Blake realized she'd have to open her big mouth again or she wasn't going to get a good night's sleep.

"What's the matter?" Mary Ellen asked as she sat down. "You look like your stomach hurts."

"It doesn't, but my head's starting to ache," Blake said. She took a deep breath. Might as well get it over with. "Mary Ellen, did you look at these catalogs?"

"Barely," Mary Ellen admitted. "I was too busy imagining myself on the cover of *Vogue*."

"Yeah, well, take a look at them and tell me where you see yourself now."

Blake shoved one of the catalogs across the table and sat back while Mary Ellen quickly turned the pages. The catalog looked like the kind of department store insert that came in the Sunday papers, but the only thing modeled in it was underwear.

"So?" Mary Ellen asked when she'd finished looking. "Modeling underwear isn't my dream, but I have to start somewhere. Mr. Seltzman called it bread-and-butter work, and I guess everybody has to do it. You don't get famous overnight."

"Bread and butter? I love it," Blake said with

111

a short laugh. "Look at this one and then tell me about bread and butter."

Blake slid a second catalog over. This one was in full color, and it featured lovely models in vivid shades of underwear, with lots of lace and appliques. The whole thing looked, to Blake, like a real sleaze job.

Mary Ellen took more time with this catalog, but when she closed it, she didn't seem worried. "So?" she said again. "I still don't see any problem. This isn't the kind of stuff I'd be doing. It's not my style, my look. Mr. Seltzman knows that."

"Did he say that?" Blake asked.

"Well, no, but — "

"But nothing," Blake broke in. "He talked about bread-and-butter work, and this is what he meant."

"Well, there's nothing wrong with this!" Mary Ellen cried. "I mean, it's just flashy, that's all. And I remember he said something about everything being legitimate. Except he said legit."

"Sure it's legit," Blake said. "But do you really want to waste three years of your life doing this?"

"It wouldn't be just this," Mary Ellen claimed.

"How do you know?" Blake pointed to the contract. "According to that, you have to do whatever work they get for you. And I'm willing to bet that Futura's more interested in how their butter tastes than how yours does."

"I can't believe this!" Mary Ellen said. She was still annoyed with Blake, but at the same time, she was beginning to have doubts about Futura.

"I'll bet you wished I'd stayed at the hotel, huh?" Blake asked.

"Yes . . . no . . . I don't know." Mary Ellen put her chin in her hands and stared wistfully at the contract. "It still doesn't seem like such a terrible deal to me. After all, it's a modeling contract, and that's what I want."

"Sure it is," Blake said softly. "But the question is, Is it the right contract for you?" She reached over and tapped a finger on the second catalog. "You haven't asked my opinion, but I'll give it to you anyway," she said with a grin. "I think you'd be wasting three years with this stuff. You know why?"

"Why?"

"Because you're too good for it, that's why." Blake sat straight up and pointed at her friend. "Bread-and-butter models are a dime a dozen. But there's only one Mary Ellen Kirkwood. Remember that."

CHAPTER

Instead of enjoying a party at Walt's, the cheerleaders found themselves staring glumly at one another in the living room of Nancy's house. They weren't downing Cokes and pretzels, either. They were sipping orange juice and nibbling half-heartedly on buttered bagels. It was ten-thirty Thursday morning.

It had been Angie's idea that they meet. The night before, she'd kept trying to reach Ardith until one-thirty. She'd started calling again at seven-thirty in the morning, and when there was still no answer two hours later, she'd called the rest of the squad, insisting that they get together to discuss the situation.

In addition to bagels, Nancy's mother had provided a variety of sweet rolls and cream-filled doughnuts. Angie hadn't touched any of the food, which was a good measure of how bad she felt.

Walt's appetite was unaffected. He was concerned, but he was also hungry. Polishing off his second roll, he leaned back on the couch and touched Angie's tense shoulder. "Loosen up, Ange," he said gently. "I really don't think there's anything to worry about. Ardith probably took a short vacation."

"She would have told us," Angie said quickly.

"Why?" Olivia asked. "She doesn't tell us every little thing she does."

"I know," Angie said. "But she let us have the whole midyear recess off without any workouts. And she didn't tell us why. But if the reason was she was going on vacation, she would have told us."

"You mean you think she needed the time to go on an interview somewhere, or maybe wrap up a deal?" Walt asked.

Angie nodded, blinking back tears.

"It makes sense," Nancy said slowly. "We've been one lousy cheerleading squad, since way before the break. Mrs. Engborg should have been tearing her hair out and calling us every name in the book. Instead, she gave us a vacation." She looked around at the faces of her friends. "What do you think, Pres? You haven't said a word since you got here."

Pres sipped some juice and shrugged. "I think we should just wait until Saturday's workout and ask Ardith," he said. "What's the point of getting hysterical when we don't know anything?"

"Nobody's getting hysterical," Nancy pointed out coldly. "We're just worried. Aren't you?" She noticed that Pres was bleary-eyed and trying not to yawn. "Maybe you don't care," she said.

"Blake's been gone two days and you were obviously out very late last night. If you don't care about her, why should the squad matter to you?"

"Not that it's any of your business, but I wasn't out anywhere last night," Pres told her. "That was a cheap shot, Nancy."

"Oh, please," Angie protested. "The last thing we need to do is fight!"

"I'm sorry, Pres," Nancy said quickly. "I shouldn't have popped off like that. I just hate not knowing."

"It's all right," Pres told her. "But like I said, there's nothing we can do right now, so why don't we just cool out till Ardith gets back?" He stood up and reached for his jacket. "Listen, guys, I've got to get going. See you Saturday."

Nancy glanced at her watch. She had to be in Hillsborough in forty-five minutes. Jimmy Michaels would be waiting for her. "I've got to go soon, too," she said with a sigh. The last thing she felt like doing was putting on a cheerful, encouraging smile, even for a spunky kid like Jimmy.

The others stood up and started putting on their coats. Olivia wrapped her long muffler around her neck and slipped her arm through Angie's. "Come on," she said brightly. "Walt and I will drop you wherever you're going."

"I'm going home," Angie said, and managed a weak smile. "I don't care what Pres says, I'm going to call Ardith every hour on the hour until I get an answer."

"Do whatever makes you feel better, Ange,"

116

Walt said, wrapping an arm around her shoulders.

Angie nodded and fumbled in her pockets for her gloves. A piece of paper fell out and she read it as they walked outside to Walt's car. The note was in Chris's handwriting.

> Dear Angie,
> When you read this, you'd better smile. If you don't, I'll give up poetry forever!
>
> > Roses are red,
> > Angie is blue,
> > If I can't cheer her up,
> > I belong in the zoo.
> > The zoo's not so bad.
> > For lions and seals,
> > But without Angie's smile,
> > My whole world is unreal.

Angie smiled, but by the time Walt and Olivia dropped her off at her house, the smile had been replaced by an uncharacteristic frown. She hurried inside and headed straight for the telephone.

"She's really upset," Walt remarked as he pulled away from the curb.

"I don't blame her," Olivia said. "I'm upset, too. But I don't think calling Ardith every hour is going to do any good. There has to be some practical way to find out where Ardith is."

"I can think of one way," Walt said, knitting his eyebrows. "I don't know how practical it is, but it'll give us something to do. It might be kind of fun, actually."

"What?"

"Go by Ardith's apartment," Walt said. "Talk to some of her neighbors, maybe even check her mailbox."

"You make it sound like private detective work," Olivia said thoughtfully.

"Mmm." Walt's eyes started to twinkle. "What do you think?"

Olivia turned to him and grinned. "Let's do it!"

Laughing, Walt pulled a quick U-turn, and as they headed toward Ardith's apartment, they passed Pres in his Porsche. Pres was too intent on his driving to notice them.

"What do you suppose is bugging him?" Walt wondered.

"It's hard to tell," Olivia said, "but I'll bet anything it's not Ardith."

Olivia was right. Pres was definitely not thinking about his cheerleading coach at that moment. His mind was on Blake Norton, as it had been from the moment she'd left for Chicago.

With an ironic smile, Pres remembered what he'd told Blake when she said she was leaving — that nothing would change while she was gone, that he'd still feel the same way about her when she returned.

The funny part was, he still *did* feel the same way about her. But Pres hadn't counted on meeting Priscilla Crandall, the extremely attractive nursery school teacher whose red hair, green eyes, and lively personality had excited him almost the minute he saw her.

Not that Priscilla Crandall had tried to flirt with him. While moving Priscilla's things, Pres had even learned that she was engaged. What's more, it didn't take a deep thinker to figure out that she was completely in love with her fiancé. No, she hadn't flirted with Pres at all. She'd managed to turn his head by simply being there.

What had Patrick said? "You recover fast, don't you." That wasn't true; Pres knew he wasn't so shallow that he could forget about Blake in the space of four hours. He hadn't forgotten about her at all, and he hadn't recovered, either. What bothered him, though, what kept him from sleeping that night, was wondering what might happen if some beautiful, lively girl who wasn't engaged came along and *did* flirt with him. Could he really hold back while Blake was in New York? Could he really live out the long-distance romance he'd worked up in his mind?

Barely noticing the scenery around him — the beautiful lake ringed with trees that would soon be lime-green with the first leaves of spring — Pres gunned the engine and tore up the drive to his house. He parked the Porsche and headed inside, noticing with relief that his father, though just back the night before from his business trip, had already left for work. No rest for the president of Tarenton Fabricators!

That was another thing, Pres thought as he climbed the stairs to his room. Tarenton Fabricators. Could he really work there, even if it did mean seeing Blake once a month?

At dinner the night before, Pres's father had talked almost nonstop about his trip to New York, with more animation in his voice than Pres had heard in a long time. But Preston Tilford II wasn't talking about Rockefeller Center or a

119

Soho art gallery. He was talking about some business deal he'd made, describing lengthy memos, working lunches, and conference-table bickering until Pres's eyes began to glaze over with boredom.

Pres knew he'd make his father the happiest man in the world by saying he wanted to join the firm and learn the ropes. He also knew, after staring at his bedroom ceiling most of the night, that he couldn't do it. Not even to see Blake.

So where did that leave his relationship with Blake? Right back where it started, just as she'd known all along. *She saw through my little fantasy from the beginning,* Pres thought, *and now I've got to tell her she was right.*

If he just hadn't been so pushy and so sure of himself, the two of them could have been having a great time together these past few days. Instead, he'd blown it, and Blake was off in Chicago while he was lying on his bed feeling like a jerk.

If Pres could have known what Blake was thinking at that moment, he might have felt better about himself.

Blake was itching to get back to Tarenton. There wasn't much time left in the midyear recess, and no matter what happened, she wanted to spend that time with Pres. She hoped he'd gotten over the urge to propose marriage, of course, but if he hadn't, she could always deal with that by making jokes. Or maybe she'd put a wad of gum in her mouth and crack it.

Pres Tilford was one terrific guy, she thought

as she stuffed clothes into her canvas carryall. Blake kept wishing she and Mary Ellen had decided to take an earlier plane. As it was, they wouldn't be getting to Tarenton until seven that night, and it wasn't even noon yet.

"What are we going to do for the rest of the day?" she asked Mary Ellen, who was busy packing, too. "I mean, look out that window. It's snowing so hard, we can't even see the lake."

"I know, and yesterday was so clear," Mary Ellen said. "Chicago weather is tricky."

"Speaking of tricky," Blake said with a laugh, "have you called good old Marty Seltzman yet?"

Mary Ellen sighed and then shook her head. "I just can't think of what to say. Maybe I should just write him a letter instead."

"No, you have to call him. You said you would and it won't look good if you don't," Blake said. "And if you really want to be professional about the whole thing, you have to write him a letter, too, thanking him."

"Yeah," Mary Ellen joked. "After all, he did offer me a 'legit' modeling job."

"Sure it's legit," Blake grinned. "But it's still sleaze. Hey, look," she went on, "you're smart to turn it down. Just keep remembering that when you call him."

Mary Ellen picked up the phone and dialed, repeating, "I'm smart to turn it down," until Futura's purring receptionist came on the line.

Mary Ellen gave her name. "I had an interview with Mr. Seltzman yesterday," she said. "I told him I'd call him today about the contract."

"I'm sorry," the receptionist said, "Mr. Seltzman can't be disturbed right now. Would you like to leave a message?"

Mary Ellen smiled in relief. She hadn't really wanted to talk to Martin Seltzman again. "Yes," she said, "would you please tell him that I . . . that my lawyer advised me not to sign such a . . . a . . ."

"Binding," Blake hissed.

". . . such a binding contract," Mary Ellen went on, "but that I appreciate his interest."

"I'll see that he gets the message, Miss Dirkwood."

"Kirkwood," Mary Ellen corrected. But the receptionist had already hung up.

"You sounded like a total professional," Blake commented as Mary Ellen went back to her packing.

"Too bad I'm not," Mary Ellen said. But she laughed as she said it. She didn't feel as bad as she'd expected. She felt frustrated, sure. After all, she'd just spent her entire savings chasing a dream that wasn't going to come true — not this time around, anyway. And now she was going home empty-handed.

Yesterday, after she and Blake had left the gelato bar, Mary Ellen had walked the rest of the way back to the hotel. Blake, still limping, had hopped onto a bus, but Mary Ellen had needed to think, so she had chosen to walk slowly, despite the cold air and rising wind.

At first, she'd been tempted to forget everything Blake had said, and to rush back to Futura with a signed contract. It was a modeling career, after all, something she wanted more than anything else in the world.

But what kind of career? That was the question she hadn't been able to stop asking herself. Three years of modeling underwear to put bread and butter on Futura's table? Was that really what she wanted?

By the time she had reached the hotel, Mary Ellen knew the answer. It wasn't what she wanted. She also knew that Blake was right. There was only one Mary Ellen Kirkwood, and she could do much better than sign three years of her life away to the Futura Modeling Agency, let alone model underwear — a thought that made her squirm.

Mary Ellen had been disappointed, but her disappointment wasn't as bitter as it had been when she'd been turned down in New York. This time, she'd been the one doing the turning down, and it had made her feel — while not good, exactly — in control of her life.

So she wasn't going home empty-handed. She still had her pride, and her ambition. She also had souvenirs. For everybody — her family, Patrick, and the rest of the cheerleaders — she'd bought T-shirts with CHICAGO! emblazoned on them in red letters.

Mary Ellen planned to give the shirts to the squad at their next workout. She knew that sometimes something as simple as a new leotard or a bright hair clip could make a difference in her attitude. She'd put on something new and suddenly feel more energetic. So with six people wearing brand new Chicago T-shirts, maybe they'd get the zip back into their routines.

The thought of the Varsity Squad raised Mary Ellen's spirits. The cheerleaders were her friends, and they were also a team. She was ready to get back to them and go to work.

CHAPTER

Walt and Olivia sat in the car and stared out at Ardith Engborg's apartment complex. The whole place looked a bit run-down — the hedges were scruffy, the pavement was cracked, and the doors needed a fresh coat of white paint.

"Which apartment is Ardith's?" Walt asked.

"I don't know," Olivia said. "I thought you knew."

"No, I don't know. I thought *you* did."

They both laughed, feeling slightly ridiculous. Their private detective work was getting off to a slow start.

"Well, it can't be that hard to find out," Olivia said finally. "The mailboxes are right there, by the doors. All we have to do is check them."

"Right," Walt agreed. "But wait a minute. What if somebody asks us what we're doing?"

"We tell them," Olivia said. "We aren't doing anything wrong, you know." She laughed again and flung her muffler around her neck. "Come on, Manners, we've got a case to solve."

"I'm right behind you, Evans," Walt quipped. "I just wish I had a trench coat. What's a P.I. without a trench coat?"

Together, the investigative team walked up the sidewalk between the hedges and began searching for a mailbox marked ENGBORG. They were serious about finding out whether their coach was deserting them, and the thought that she might be was not a laughing matter. But sneaking from mailbox to mailbox, peering over their shoulders as if they were being followed, and whispering like conspirators struck them both as extremely funny. They kept erupting in giggles over the situation.

"Face it," Olivia said, "we're a couple of hopeless amateurs."

"Not so fast, partner," Walt told her. "Look here." He triumphantly pointed to a mailbox with Ardith's name on it.

"Great, we found it!" Olivia said excitedly.

They giggled again and slapped hands, celebrating their first success. "This is fun," Walt said, "but what do we do now?"

"Oh, right, the case! Well. . . ." Olivia glanced around surreptitiously, then casually flipped open the mailbox and peered inside. "Empty," she reported.

"Ah ha. And what can we deduce from that, Evans?"

"One of three things, Manners," Olivia said. "A neighbor is taking in Mrs. Engborg's mail for her and already did it, or Mrs. Engborg didn't get any mail today, or the mail hasn't come yet." She stopped, frowning. "Of course, I don't know what we'd do with the mail if we *did* get our hands on it."

"We'll figure that out later." Walt checked his watch. "It's only one-thirty," he said. "I'll bet the mail hasn't come. We don't get ours till about three."

"Yeah, but you live way out in the sticks," Olivia reminded him.

"True." Walt thought for a second, and scratched his head. "Like I said, what do we do now?"

"I don't know, but we can't just give up." Olivia peeked inside the mailbox again, as if some clue might have magically appeared there. As she did, a nearby door opened and an elderly woman carrying a Chihuahua stepped outside.

Flashing a suspicious look at the two cheerleaders, the women asked, "Can I help you with something?"

Walt cleared his throat and the tiny dog immediately started yapping. "We were looking for Mrs. Engborg," Walt said over the noise. "Ardith Engborg. You probably know her."

"We're from Tarenton High," Olivia explained. "Mrs. Engborg's our cheerleading coach."

The woman's face relaxed and she set the dog down on the sidewalk, where it hopped on its hind feet in a circle, yipping excitedly.

"Hush, Ralph!" the woman said. She turned to the cheerleaders. "Mrs. Engborg's out of town."

"Oh, too bad," Walt said innocently. "She didn't happen to say where she was going, did she?"

"No, she didn't. We're neighbors, but we're not all that close," the woman told him. "We do help each other out, though. I collect her mail whenever she's away, she collects mine. Hush, Ralph! Speaking of the mail. . . ." She looked in her own mailbox and clicked her tongue. "It gets here later and later every day!"

"Maybe you just didn't get any," Walt said.

"Oh, that can't be. This is the day for my social security check."

Ralph was working himself into such a frenzy that Olivia was afraid he might self-destruct. "I don't think your dog likes us too much," she remarked.

"Oh, no, he's just a spoiled baby. Can't stand to wait an extra minute when it's time for his walk," the woman said. "Is there a message you'd like to leave for Mrs. Engborg?"

"No, thanks," Walt said quickly. "We'll see her when she gets back. Thanks, anyway. Nice talking to you."

Nodding pleasantly, the woman headed down the sidewalk with Ralph jumping and yapping at her heels like a windup toy.

Walt and Olivia looked at each other, their eyes sparkling. "You know what this means, don't you?" Olivia asked.

"Yep. A stakeout!" Walt grabbed her hand. "Come on, let's wait in the car for the mailman. It's freezing out here. If your mother drove by and saw you, she'd never let you out of the house again."

"I have a confession to make," Olivia said after they were settled in the car. "Here we are, trying to find out if Mrs. Engborg's leaving Tarenton High, and I'm actually enjoying myself."

"Boy, am I glad you said that!" Walt told her. "Because you know what? I feel the same way. I'm having a great time. This is better than ice-skating, you have to admit."

"Well, at least it's different," Olivia agreed. "See? You were looking for something exciting to happen, and it did."

"Yeah. You think we ought to go into business together?" Walt suggested. "I can see it now — 'Evans and Manners: Four Private Eyes for the Price of Two.'"

"I think we should wait until we solve our first case before we start advertising," Olivia said dryly.

"You're right." Walt grinned and held out his hand. "Why don't you come over here and help keep me warm while we wait?"

Olivia slid over and the two of them snuggled in the chilly car, waiting for the mailman and feeling happier together than they had in a long time.

How strange, Olivia thought. It took the possibility of Mrs. Engborg leaving to bring us closer. Playing detective has made us a team again. It's a little weird, but who cares? Kissing's more fun than arguing or worrying. We never have any trouble arguing, and we can always worry, if and when we find out that Vanessa's rumor is true.

They started worrying sooner than Olivia expected. From the car, they watched the mailman drop several envelopes into Mrs. Engborg's box. Then, while Walt kept an eye out in case Ralph's owner returned and caught them in the act of rifling through her neighbor's mail, Olivia pulled out the letters and quickly read the return addresses.

"Find anything?" Walt called from between the hedges.

Olivia swallowed hard and held up one of the envelopes. Walt left his post and trotted up to her. "It's from Carleton College, see?" she said. "From the athletic department." Her voice was a little shaky. Carleton was a wealthy private college in another part of the state. It would definitely be a step up for their coach.

"It's pure coincidence," Walt told her. "Teachers get stuff from other schools all the time."

"But this is a college," Olivia pointed out.

"So maybe Mrs. Engborg's going back to school or something."

"Maybe." Olivia looked doubtful. But she wasn't ready to do anything as drastic as taking the letter and steaming it open. Sighing, she put the envelope back in the mailbox. "Now what?"

Walt saw that she was upset. "Tea or coffee," he said, hoping to lighten her mood. "I don't know about you, but this stakeout has made me appreciate the simple things of life. Like a warm drink on a cold day." He took her hand, smiling.

"Don't think about it now. Let's go warm up first. *Then* we can think about it."

Think about it. That's all Nancy had been able to do since she'd first heard the news. Driving to Hillsborough, she'd kept telling herself that it was simply not true. Vanessa Barlow had struck again, that was all. There was nothing to worry about.

Still, Nancy worried. What if it *was* true? What if Mrs. Engborg was leaving Tarenton High? She had every right to. She'd put in a lot of time, turning the squad into the best cheerleading team in the tri-state region. She'd given them her all, and what had they done? Gotten lazy. Performed like sleepwalkers. Made excuses — they were tired, the weather was lousy. They'd let Mrs. Engborg down. This wasn't the first time they'd let her down, but it might be the last.

Stop it, Nancy told herself as she drove up to the junior college. You can't get depressed over a cheerleading team, of all things. What would Eric say? Eric worked with people who had real problems. What would he think of somebody who fell apart over cheerleading?

As Nancy changed into her swimsuit and joined Jimmy Michaels in the pool, she tried to convince herself that being a cheerleader didn't rank very high in the great scheme of things. It was a pleasant pastime, nothing more.

Nancy didn't convince herself, of course. She knew what being on the squad meant to her. When she'd first transferred here, she'd been completely out of it. Part of it was being the only Jewish girl around, and part of it was simply being the "new kid on the block," trying to find a place for herself at Tarenton High.

Then she'd made the squad. From then on, whenever the group worked together, Nancy felt like she'd come home.

"Nancy?" Jimmy, a freckled-faced towhead with huge brown eyes, finally brought Nancy out of her reverie with his questioning voice.

"I'm sorry, Jimmy. What did you say?"

Jimmy was still holding onto the edge of the pool, panting a little. "I said, how long have I been kicking?"

Nancy checked the clock. Jimmy was supposed to kick for three minutes. While she'd been feeling sorry for herself, eight minutes had gone by. No wonder he was winded.

"I think you set a record, Jimmy," she said, feeling ashamed. "Why don't you take a break now? You've earned it."

She helped him out of the pool, then walked over to Eric, who had just come in. As always, she noticed his beautiful, muscular body, but today the sight of it didn't cheer her up.

"How's he doing?" Eric asked, indicating Jimmy with a lift of his chin.

"A whole lot better than I am," Nancy admitted. She explained how she'd let Jimmy work longer than she should have. "I can't believe I just ignored him for almost eight minutes."

"It didn't hurt him," Eric said, putting his hand on her bare shoulder. "But you're worried about more than Jimmy, aren't you?"

It was amazing, Nancy thought, how well he read her. Nodding miserably, she told him about Mrs. Engborg's possible defection. "Dumb, huh?" she said when she finished. "Getting so depressed about cheerleading that I mess up the really important things, like Jimmy's therapy."

Eric didn't speak for a minute, and Nancy knew he was working out what he wanted to say. He almost never talked off the top of his head; he liked to think things through.

Finally, he ran a hand through his shiny black hair. "Don't be so hard on yourself," he said quietly. "Sure, cheerleading's not a life-and-death situation, but it's important to you."

"But it seems so shallow compared to what you're doing," Nancy said.

"Like I said, you're being too hard on yourself," Eric told her. "You do volunteer work here, don't forget. But that's not the point. If the squad's important to you, then it's important, period."

"Well. . . ." Nancy shrugged. "Of course, if Mrs. Engborg leaves, there probably won't be a squad."

"Why not? You'll get a new coach, that's all. You'll start over."

A new coach? Nancy hadn't thought that far ahead, and the prospect was not thrilling. Who could possibly replace Mrs. Engborg?

"I see people starting over here every day," Eric went on, pointing to Jimmy again. "If they can do it, you can do it."

Nancy realized he was right. In his quiet way, Eric had put everything into perspective. If

133

Ardith left, they'd start over with somebody new. That wouldn't be easy, but the squad could stick together and do it. She reached up and touched Eric's cheek with her finger. "Did I ever tell you you're terrific?"

"You might have mentioned it, but I don't mind if you repeat yourself. Hey, that's better," Eric said, as Nancy laughed. "Keep smiling. One thing's for sure — there's no sense crying *before* the milk gets spilled."

While the team of Evans and Manners was discussing Ardith's mail over cups of tea at Walt's house, Angie was unenthusiastically checking the mail at *her* house. Bills, mostly, plus a folded sheet of notepaper with something bulky stuck inside.

Opening it, Angie found another of Chris's poems:

> Angie is dandy,
> Angie is great.
> I'll give her some candy
> If she'll be my date!

Taped to the note was a grape lollipop. Angie smiled fondly. Chris was really stretching his poetry by writing this stuff to cheer her up.

The poem did cheer her up, but only for a few minutes. Unlike Nancy, Angie wasn't ashamed of feeling miserable about cheerleading. She didn't need anyone to tell her that it was all right to take it seriously. She just needed to know what was happening. The uncertainty was terrible.

As she stepped back into her warm house, the phone rang. Angie grabbed it.

"Angie? It's Olivia."

"Oh, hi."

"Listen, I wanted to tell you not to keep calling Mrs. Engborg," Olivia said. "Walt and I went to her apartment complex and a neighbor told us she's out of town."

"Did the neighbor tell you where she went?" Angie asked.

"She didn't know. Look, Angie," Olivia went on, "Mrs. Engborg called a practice for Saturday. You know she'll be there and then we can find out what's happening." Olivia and Walt had decided not to mention the letter from Carleton College. Angie was upset enough. "Angie?"

"Okay," Angie said. "I guess we'll just have to wait for Saturday. Thanks for calling."

"Sure. Wait." Olivia paused and then came back on the line. "Walt wants to know if you and Chris will go to the movies with us tonight."

"Oh. Well, Chris asked me out, sort of." Angie looked at the poem she was still carrying. "But I don't know if I want to go anywhere yet."

"Come on, Angie." Olivia tried to sound bright and chipper. "It'll be fun. We'll go for pizza after. You can't turn that down!"

"Okay," Angie said indifferently. "I'll talk to Chris and call you later. Bye, Livvy."

The phone rang again as soon as Angie hung up.

"Hello?"

"Do we have a date?" Chris demanded with a laugh.

"Do I get to keep the lollipop if I turn you down?" Angie asked.

"No way," Chris joked. "Come on, Angie. I can't stand to see you like this. Would it help if I stood on my head?"

Angie smiled into the phone. "How about doing a cartwheel?"

"Anything!"

"Oh, Chris, I'm sorry," Angie told him. "I know I'm a real drag right now, but I can't help it."

"I understand, really."

"We were invited to go to the movies with Olivia and Walt tonight," Angie said. "But I don't really feel like it."

"Anything's okay with me," Chris said. "You just want me to come over?"

Angie ran a hand through her hair. It needed a good brushing. "I look awful," she warned him. "And you know what kind of mood I'm in."

"I'll take my chances with you anytime," Chris said softly. "See you at eight."

As bad as Angie felt, the thought of being with Chris did help to perk her up a bit. Enough, anyway, to want to look good for him.

She went into the bathroom and studied her face in the mirror. "You were right," she told her reflection. "You look awful."

Angie's shining face rarely needed makeup, but today it looked dull. Even her lips, normally a natural red, were pale. She bit them and watched the color appear. That was something she'd seen Mary Ellen do a hundred times in the locker room just before a game.

Mary Ellen! Angie thought suddenly. Mary Ellen didn't even know about Mrs. Engborg. What was she going to think when she heard what Vanessa had said?

Angie knew that Mary Ellen always had one eye on her future. But she also knew that the other eye was firmly fixed on the Varsity Squad. In her own way, Mary Ellen loved cheerleading as much as Angie did. What was she going to do when she came back and discovered that their coach might be moving on?

CHAPTER

When Mary Ellen walked through the gate at the Tarenton airport Thursday night, the first person she saw was Patrick Henley. He was standing exactly the same way he had when she'd left for Chicago — hands stuffed in the pockets of his jeans, feet slightly apart, head up, eyes on her face.

He looked wonderful, Mary Ellen thought. She'd said some awful things to him before she'd left, and still he was here, waiting for her. The smile on his face and the light in his eyes warmed her deep inside, driving out the chill of disappointment over the Chicago fiasco.

Pres was waiting, too, for Blake. But Mary Ellen simply waved at Pres and then walked straight to Patrick and kissed him on the cheek.

"How'd it go?" he asked immediately.

With a rueful smile, Mary Ellen gave him a

thumbs-down signal. "I'll explain later," she said. "Right now, I just want to go home." She searched his face, hoping she wouldn't detect any relief there, any pleasure that she hadn't succeeded.

Patrick was relieved, but not because she'd failed. She wouldn't be Mary Ellen if she didn't want to be a model. She'd be somebody else, somebody he wouldn't want. "I'm sorry, Mary Ellen," he said sincerely. "You don't look too broken up, though."

"I am and I'm not," Mary Ellen said. "I could have had the job, but it wasn't . . . quite what I was looking for."

"Not quite?" Blake hooted with laughter as she and Pres joined them. "It was pure, out-and-out sleaze, that's what it was."

"What do you mean?" Pres asked.

Blake rolled her eyes and lowered her voice. "Modeling underwear," she whispered out of the side of her mouth. "Personally, I think the whole thing was a front for something suspicious."

"Oh, Blake, it was not," Mary Ellen said, laughing. She tried to imitate Martin Seltzman's voice: " 'It was legit, strictly legit.' "

"What's wrong with underwear?" Pres asked with a grin. "Everybody wears it."

"But not everybody models it," Mary Ellen shot back. "Not me, that's for sure!"

Still laughing, the four walked outside and got into the moving van. Mary Ellen sat up front with Patrick. As they headed into Tarenton she thought again how glad she'd been to see his face, how lucky she was to have him waiting for her.

In some ways they were worlds apart: She wanted a glamorous life away from Tarenton; he was already building a very unglamorous life right here in the town she wanted to leave. But they were both ambitious; they both knew what they wanted and they both chased their dreams. In some ways, they were very much alike.

Could their two worlds ever become one? Mary Ellen didn't think so, but at the moment, she didn't care. Patrick was here, beside her, and for now that was enough.

She reached out and touched his hand. "I'm glad to see you," she said.

Patrick briefly let go of the wheel and squeezed her finger. "Glad to see you, Mary Ellen."

In the back, Blake kept up a steady stream of chatter about her parents, and Chicago — "Nice, but it's not New York" — and made some more withering comments about the Futura Modeling Agency. She was using her talk as a cover for her nerves. She wanted her last couple of days in Tarenton to be two of the greatest days she'd ever spent, but she still didn't know where the situation stood with Pres. She could hardly ask him now, with Patrick and Mary Ellen up front and the panel between the driver's seat and the back wide open. So she let her mouth run on as if it had a mind of its own.

Pres was as edgy as Blake. How could he tell her she'd been right about him without sounding like a guy whose feelings were skin deep? Every time he imagined saying, "Blake, I was wrong.

The timing's all off," the words seemed hollow, his personality superficial.

Instead of covering his nervousness with small talk, Pres kept quiet, listening, but barely responding, to Blake's nonstop chitchat.

Finally, Blake wound down and the van grew quiet. Pres felt a sudden urge to break the silence, and he said the first thing that came into his mind. "Hey, you know what, Mary Ellen?"

"What?"

"Mrs. Engborg might be leaving Tarenton High."

Mary Ellen turned halfway around in her seat. "She *what*?"

"Might be leaving," Pres repeated, and relayed Vanessa's news.

"It isn't true," Mary Ellen said firmly. "Vanessa devotes what brains she has to thinking up lies. You know that."

"You could be right," Pres agreed. "We'll have to ask Mrs. Engborg on Saturday."

"Why wait till Saturday?" Mary Ellen wanted to know. "Why not call her now?"

"Angie's been trying, but it seems our coach has mysteriously flown the coop."

"Don't be cute, Pres," Mary Ellen said. "Just tell me what you mean."

"I mean Mrs. Engborg's away, and nobody knows where," he said. "So we'll have to wait until Saturday's workout to ask her."

Blake spoke up. "She doesn't strike me as the kind of person who'd skip out on you guys."

"She's not," Pres agreed. "She'd tell us, *then* she'd leave."

141

"She's not leaving!" Mary Ellen insisted. But her thoughts were boiling as she went through all the reasons why Ardith Engborg might leave the squad. She came up with the same reasons Nancy had: their laziness, their excuses, their recent lack of spirit. They were good reasons, and Mary Ellen's mood, which had been so high, took a giant dip.

What would she be without the squad? Until she made it as a model, she'd be a nothing, a nobody — that's what. Mary Ellen could sometimes be brutally honest with herself, and she knew that a big part of what she loved about being a cheerleader was the status it gave her in everyone else's eyes. She liked that. She liked being admired and envied.

But there was more to her than that. Before leaving Chicago, she realized how lucky she was to have such a great team of friends to go back to. The team meant more than all the praise and envy in the world, and knowing the group was waiting for her made turning down Martin Seltzman almost easy.

But now what? If Ardith really was leaving, there wouldn't be a team. Mary Ellen wondered if she'd come back from Chicago to nothing, and the thought that she might have made her angry. She'd save her sadness for later, if the news did turn out to be true. For now, she was furious.

By the time the van reached Pres's house, Blake's mouth was tired of moving. It was just as well, she thought, since she'd actually run out of things to say. That was something of a first!

She waved good-bye to Mary Ellen and Patrick, and taking Pres's arm, led him into the house, through the wide main hall, past the dining room, and into the family room. It was the coziest place in the house, and as far as she was concerned, the only room in which she felt comfortable.

"Let's talk," she said bluntly, looking Pres in the eye. "You go first."

Pres grinned. "Read any good books lately?"

"No fair," Blake said, grinning back. "You know what I mean."

"Okay, okay." He sat down on one of the soft chairs and stared at her for a moment. She was so terrific. Why did they have to live a thousand miles apart? "Okay," he said again, taking a deep breath. "It took me a while, but I finally saw what you meant. About me not seeing *you*, Blake Norton. I mean, I knew it all along, but I just ignored it. You don't want a long-distance romance. And I finally realized something else." Pres paused and breathed deeply again. "I don't want one, either."

Blake started to say something, but Pres held up his hand. "You've got to know, though," he said, "that I'm still crazy about you. If you lived in Tarenton or I lived in New York, you'd have to use one of your karate chops to get rid of me. And even that might not work."

"Oh, yeah?" Blake asked with a smile.

"Yeah," Pres said. "Anyway, what I'm trying to say is, you were right. I jumped into this whole thing without even looking. It's like I made two

143

reservations for a trip around the world and forgot to ask if you wanted to go."

"You forgot to ask yourself if you wanted to go, too," Blake said. "But you don't. It's just not the right time, huh?"

"The timing couldn't be worse," Pres admitted softly. "I'm sorry, Blake."

Well, he finally came to his senses, Blake told herself. How do you feel now? It wasn't an easy question to answer. She was relieved, sure, because she knew she'd been right. Their relationship had no place to go — not yet, anyway. Still, she couldn't help wishing that she'd been wrong. Boy, did she wish it!

Pres had been staring at the carpet, waiting for Blake to say something. When she didn't respond, he finally looked at her. "Blake, what is it?" he asked, peering at her face. "Do you have something in your eyes?"

"No, why?"

"Because you're blinking like crazy," he said.

"That's because I'm trying not to cry, you dope!" Blake kept on blinking. "Quick, say something funny before I blubber like a baby."

Instead, Pres got up and put his arms around her. "I love you, Blake," he whispered. "Maybe someday things'll be right for us. Let's make a date for another time and another place, okay?"

"You're on." Blake pushed away a tear that was threatening to slide down her cheek. "Okay," she said briskly, "I've got exactly two days before I fly out of here. Let's have some fun!"

* * *

On Friday, Pres and Blake devoted themselves to having fun. They ate breakfast at the Pancake House, went to the nearly empty zoo and watched the elephants eat *their* own breakfast, and took a long drive into the country. They talked of everything but the future. What lay ahead of them just didn't seem as important as what was happening at the moment.

While Blake and Pres were enjoying themselves, the team of Evans and Manners moved their investigation to the halls of Tarenton High. They hoped that Mrs. Oetjen or Dr. Barlow might be there to tell them that Vanessa's rumor was totally false. All they found was a sweaty basketball team, practicing for Monday's game against Deep River, and the drama club, rehearsing for the spring musical. Their investigation was going nowhere, and they realized that they'd have to wait until tomorrow to get to the bottom of the mystery.

Also on Friday, Angie received Chris's longest and most ambitious piece of doggerel, stuck in the middle of the evening newspaper:

There once was a coach so fine,
Her squad thought she was divine.
And when Ardith left,
The kids were bereft,
They could do nothing but pine.

But one day the same coach so fine,
Returned on United Airlines.
Said the squad, "Where were you?"
Said the coach, "Katmandu.
Time to work, get up now — get in line!"

145

As Angie started to go back in the house, Chris ran up the porch steps and wrapped his arms around her. "Not bad, huh?" he said. "I wrote it in three minutes flat."

"It sounds like it!" Angie broke into her first genuine laugh in two days. "Chris, I'm sorry! But please, don't try to cheer me up anymore. This stuff is awful!"

Chris wasn't the least bit insulted. "I knew it would work," he said with a smile. "Bad poetry'll do it every time. That's what I wanted to do, Angie — make you laugh. Laughing always helps."

Chris was right; laughing did help. And on Saturday, as Mary Ellen passed out her Chicago T-shirts right before the workout, the squad got another good laugh.

They were all trying on their T-shirts when Vanessa Barlow sauntered by.

"Oh, how cute!" she remarked, eyeing the cheap cotton shirts. "You've all decided to be tacky together!" Pushing her dark satiny hair back, she eyed Mary Ellen. "Well?" she asked. "What are you doing back in Tarenton? I thought for sure you'd be modeling in Chicago by now. Don't tell me you weren't hired."

While Mary Ellen was trying to think of a biting comeback, Blake spoke up. "Vanessa Barlow!" she said, as if she'd been dying to see her. "Am I glad you showed up. You know, I tried to tell Mary Ellen that she wasn't Futura's type, but she wouldn't listen to me. She just had to go on that interview and get turned down."

146

"Oh, too bad." Vanessa clicked her tongue and tried to look sorry for Mary Ellen.

"Yeah, well, what do you expect?" Blake went on. "I mean, Futura is one classy agency. They've got wholesome girls like Mary Ellen coming out of their ears. What they're looking for is the more exotic type. Like you."

"Oh?" Vanessa smiled at Blake as if she'd suddenly discovered a long-lost friend.

"Right," Blake said, rummaging in her canvas bag. "Here. Here's Martin Seltzman's card — he's the head of Futura." She pressed the card into Vanessa's hand and gave Mary Ellen a surreptitious wink. "Mary Ellen wasn't what they were looking for, but I just know you'll be perfect."

Vanessa studied the card, gave Mary Ellen a superior smile, and strolled off.

The cheerleaders, who knew all about the "underground underwear deal," as Walt had dubbed it, broke into hysterics the minute Vanessa was out of sight.

"Thanks, Blake," Mary Ellen said. "I wasn't sure what to say to her."

"Hey, don't thank me. I enjoyed it," Blake told her. "I just wish I could be around when Vanessa finds out what Futura's all about."

Still laughing, the squad trooped into the gym and began warming up. But when Ardith arrived, the laughter died.

Ardith Engborg hated to admit it, but she was tired. It had been a long five days, and she was more in the mood for a massage than a workout.

Her fatigue didn't show, of course. She strode into the gym with all her usual briskness, took her seat on the bleachers, and surveyed her squad.

The six faces staring back at her were very different, but at the moment, they had one thing in common: They all wore extremely unfriendly expressions.

What now? Ardith wondered. When I left them, they looked bored, now they look ready to attack.

She eyed them again. There was no doubt about it, they were angry about something. Angie was the only one who didn't look mad, and she looked ready to cry.

Ardith tried a joke. "I see somebody's been to Chicago," she remarked.

It didn't get a laugh.

"Okay," she said. "Let's try 'They Can Run.'" Maybe their anger will give them some energy, at least, she thought to herself.

The cheerleaders got in position and began:

"They can run, but they can't hide,
We've got the winners on our side!
Tarenton's steppin' high,
Ready to fly,
Lookin' good. . . ."

The cheerleaders tore through the routine the way a bulldozer tears through the earth. Their smiles were brittle, their movements were sharp and angular. It was supposed to be a snappy, happy routine, but instead it came out like a drill march.

"Hold it!" Ardith called out. What on earth was wrong with them? Granted, they had energy, but it was hardly the positive kind. She sat back and surveyed them again. "Who's going to tell me what's on your minds?" she asked. "I feel like I'm under fire."

No one said anything for a minute. Then Mary Ellen spoke up. "Mrs. Engborg," she said, "we heard that you might be leaving Tarenton. Someone overheard you telling Dr. Barlow that it was time for you to move on. We'd like to know if it's true."

Ardith stared at them in disbelief. Then, shaking her head, she said, "I won't even bother to ask how you found out —"

"You mean it's true?" Angie interrupted. "You went out of town to find another job?"

"No, Angie, I went out of town to visit my uncle. He's been sick," Ardith told her. "And as for 'moving on,' I was speaking of moving on to a different apartment." She glanced at Pres, who was studying the ceiling. "As a matter of fact, I just signed a new lease, and I was thinking of hiring you and Patrick to move me. Now, I'm not so sure."

"Why?" Pres asked.

"Given your mood," Ardith remarked, "you might break all my furniture." She smiled briefly. "So. Now that we have everything cleared up, suppose we all just get back to work."

Grinning and giggling, they started the cheer. But their relief was so great, their limbs had turned to rubber. When Pres lifted Olivia, she felt like a rag doll; Mary Ellen and Nancy, doing parallel back walkovers, crashed into each other and wound up in a tangle of arms and legs; Angie's cartwheel turned into a somersault; and Walt's stag leap was simply a high hop. No one could stop laughing.

Ardith shook her head again, smiling to herself. The squad looked perfectly awful, but their spirit was back, and with some good hard work, they'd be in shape again. There was no way she'd give up on these cheerleaders.

"Okay," she called out again. "Get the laughs out of your systems." After they'd flopped onto the floor, she said, "I want you to know, by the way, that I'm flattered by your concern. But since I'm not leaving Tarenton, do me a favor."

"Anything," Walt said.

Ardith clapped her hands. "Get to work!"

"They can run, but they can't hide,
We've got the winners on our side!
Tarenton's steppin' high,
Ready to fly.

"Lookin' good,
We knew you would!
They can run, but they can't hide,
The winners are on Tarenton's side!"

150

After long weeks of going through the motions — after what seemed like even longer days of worrying about their future as a team — the six cheerleaders were looking good again.

Who nearly ruins the fabulous cheerleading clinic? Read Cheerleaders #19, MAKING IT.

CHEERLEADERS™

Join the Team!

They're talented. They're fabulous-looking. They're winners! And they've got what you want! Don't miss any of these exciting CHEERLEADERS books!

Watch for these titles! $2.25 each

- ☐ QI 33402-6 **Trying Out** *Caroline B. Cooney*
- ☐ QI 33403-4 **Getting Even** *Christopher Pike*
- ☐ QI 33404-2 **Rumors** *Caroline B. Cooney*
- ☐ QI 33405-0 **Feuding** *Lisa Norby*
- ☐ QI 33406-9 **All the Way** *Caroline B. Cooney*
- ☐ QI 33407-7 **Splitting** *Jennifer Sarasin*

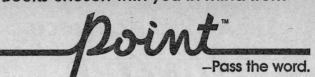